THE DRAGON IN THE VOLCANO

DRAGON KEEPERS

BOOK 1
THE DRAGON IN THE SOCK DRAWER

BOOK 2
THE DRAGON IN THE DRIVEWAY

BOOK 3
THE DRAGON IN THE LIBRARY

BOOK 4
THE DRAGON IN THE VOLCANO

DRAGON KEEPERS BOOK 4

THE DRAGON
IN THE
VOLCANO

KATE KLIMO

with illustrations
by
JOHN SHROADES

Random House 🏠 New York

For Mallory Loehr,
Dragon Keeper extraordinaire

Text copyright © 2011 by Kate Klimo
Jacket and interior illustrations copyright © 2011 by John Shroades

Visit us on the Web! www.randomhouse.com/kids

Educators and librarians, for a variety of teaching tools, visit us at
www.randomhouse.com/teachers

For more Dragon Keepers fun, go to FoundaDragon.org

Library of Congress Cataloging-in-Publication Data
Klimo, Kate.
The dragon in the volcano / Kate Klimo; with illustrations by John Shroades.—
1st ed.   p. cm. — (Dragon Keepers ; bk. 4)
Summary: Emmy the dragon is maturing and growing too large—and bored—
for her quarters, but when she disappears her Keepers, cousins Jesse and Daisy,
follow her trail to the Fiery Realm in hopes of bringing her home.
ISBN 978-0-375-86692-0 (trade)—ISBN 978-0-375-96692-7 (lib. bdg.)—
ISBN 978-0-375-89723-8 (ebook)
[1. Dragons—Fiction.   2. Magic—Fiction.   3. Lost and found possessions—Fiction.
4. Volcanoes—Fiction.   5. Cousins—Fiction.]   I. Shroades, John, ill.   II. Title.
PZ7.K67896Drv 2011   [Fic]—dc22   2010014970

Printed in the United States of America
10 9 8 7 6 5 4 3 2 1
First Edition

CONTENTS

THE WORLD
IS TALKING TO US.
EVERYTHING IN IT
HAS A STORY TO TELL.
ALL WE HAVE TO DO
IS SIT QUIETLY
AND LISTEN.
THIS STORY BEGINS
WITH A FIRE DRILL. . . .

CHAPTER ONE

FIRE DRILL

Dear Mom and Dad, This will be short
because I am in computer lab, waiting for
Ms. Lasky to come. How are things in
Tanzania? Uncle Joe measured us yesterday,
and I grew one whole inch! Did you find any

more pit vipers in your well? It's pretty chilly here. Aunt Maggie took us to buy winter coats yesterday. Mine is red plaid. It is my very first real winter coat since I was about two, I think! School is good. Ms. Lasky is the nicest teacher in the fifth grade and maybe in the universe. She doesn't mind it when Daisy and I hang out together, so long as we don't talk *too* much during class or pass notes. School lunch is GREAT. Today we had Chicken Surprise. Daisy says the surprise is that anyone believes it is really food. But I ate all of mine and most of hers, too. Aunt Maggie jokes that if Uncle Joe ever gets tired of being a geologist, he can always go to work cooking in the school cafeteria. This week, we pick our topics for science fair projects. Daisy already has hers. I'm not sure about mine yet. I guess the only problem with school is that Emmy gets bored during the day when we're not around.

Jesse didn't tell his parents that Emmy, his and Daisy's dragon who masqueraded as a sheepdog, was *so* bored that she had taken to sneaking out of the garage and running loose around the neighborhood. Sometimes, she even followed them to school. Other times, she disappeared for hours and wouldn't say where she had been. Daisy was afraid that Emmy was off hunting squirrels and bunnies and other defenseless woodland creatures. When Emmy had started flying, she had switched from eating foods like cheese and cabbage to eating meat. The more meat she ate, the bigger she got. She was almost too big for the garage now, which was a major worry. Where were the Dragon Keepers going to keep their dragon when she didn't fit in the garage?

Jesse was just signing off when a loud buzzing noise brought him to his feet. He looked around. All the other kids were standing up in their places and looking just as startled as he was. The next moment, Ms. Lasky came into the room and clapped her hands. "Fire drill, kids! Line up along the front wall for a head count."

Jesse found a place next to Daisy against the blackboard.

"I think it might be a real fire," Daisy said, her blue eyes shiny with excitement.

When Ms. Lasky had finished counting, she said, "Okay, kids, follow me. We're going to *walk*— okay?—not run, down the hall, out the fire exit, and line up on the sidewalk in front of the school. You all know the drill."

"Why do you think it's a real fire?" Jesse whispered as they walked swiftly down the hall. Kids from other classes were pouring out of their rooms in orderly lines.

Daisy tugged on one of her pale-blond braids. Her ears were bright pink and a little pointy. Her nose was pink, too, and right now, it was twitching like a rabbit's. "Because I smell something burning—don't you?"

Jesse sniffed and shrugged. To him, that was the way October smelled in America, like burning leaves. He had lived in hot countries his whole life before moving in with his cousin Daisy's family last spring. He liked the autumn almost as much as the spring. He liked the way the trees, with their leaves of bright yellow and red and orange, seemed to be lit up from within, like giant lanterns. He even liked the way it got dark early and the lights in the houses along their street winked on as Jesse and Daisy walked home after school.

Uncle Joe had started to make fires in the living room fireplace at night. Jesse loved sitting on the hearth and staring into the dancing flames. He and Daisy would sit before the fire and sing one of the rounds they had learned in chorus, first Jesse, then Daisy joining in:

"Fire's burning! Fire's burning!
Draw nearer! Draw nearer!
In the gloaming! In the gloaming!
Come sing and be merry!"

By now, all of the kids from kindergarten through fifth grade were lined up on the sidewalk outside the school. The kids who had been at recess had their coats on. The kids who had been in gym class were shivering in their gym uniforms, and the kids who had been in art class were wearing their smocks. They all stood quietly in their groups and stared at the school building as if they expected it to burst into flames at any second.

Suddenly, the public address speakers crackled as the voice of Ms. Goodman, the principal, announced, "This has been a fire drill. Please wait to return to your classrooms until the buzzer sounds again."

Daisy's shoulders slumped in disappointment.

The next moment, they heard an eruption of laughter coming from the third graders standing on the corner.

"What's going on now?" Daisy wondered.

Suddenly, their dragon, Emmy, in sheepdog form, came trotting around the corner of the building with a nozzle clenched in her mouth. She proudly dragged behind her the green garden hose belonging to Mr. Fine, the school janitor. Then Uncle Joe came barreling into view, his long, graying ponytail flying behind him as he frantically waved Emmy's leash in the air.

"Emmy, put that hose down this instant!" he called to her.

Now everyone was laughing, even Ms. Goodman, who had come outside to see what all the commotion was about.

Emmy stopped running and gave Uncle Joe a chance to catch up with her. Then she began running circles around him, and it wasn't long before Daisy's father was wrapped like a mummy up to his knees. When Emmy ran out of hose, she dropped the nozzle on the ground and sat in front of Uncle Joe. Her stub of a tail wagged eagerly, her long, pink, forked tongue lolling out of her mouth.

The only person who wasn't laughing, other than Uncle Joe and Jesse and Daisy, was their classmate Dewey Forbes. "Your dog is an ill-mannered upstart," he said. "My Loretta would never do anything like this. That's because poodles have manners. I've made a study of it, and I have concluded that Emmy must not really be a purebred sheepdog. She must have something else mixed in there . . . like *Devil Dog!*" Now Dewey snickered and snorted.

Daisy leveled a dead-eyed stare at Dewey.

Jesse shook his head sadly. What could he say? Emmy's behavior was nothing to brag about. The fact was that Emmy was an excellent dragon but, lately at least, a very bad dog.

"She's just bored," said Daisy, "because we're in school all day."

"Maybe you should try crating her," said Dewey. "As a training method, crating has a high degree of proven success."

Jesse shuddered at the thought of cooping Emmy up like that. They had nailed together two wooden packing crates to make a nest for her, filled with their rolled-up socks. But only yesterday, she had cracked her nest because she was so big.

Mr. Fine and Ms. Goodman were untangling Uncle Joe from the hose. When they were done, Uncle Joe snapped the leash onto Emmy's purple collar and walked her back around the corner of the building to take her home. The all-clear buzzer sounded. One by one, the classes began to file back into the building.

As Ms. Lasky's class began to move, Jesse caught sight of Uncle Joe's beat-up old truck heading down the road in the direction of home. Emmy was sitting in the front seat, peering forlornly out the back window. Just then, Jesse caught a glimpse of High Peak, looming over the tops of the trees. It was the extinct volcano where he had found the thunder egg from which Emmy had hatched. A cloud was snagged on the mountain's snowcapped summit, looking remarkably like a wisp of smoke. Or was it a *real* wisp of smoke?

They didn't have any after-school activities, so Jesse and Daisy headed home when the last lesson was over. Emmy was waiting for them in the garage. They had run out of animals to compare her with for size. She was bigger than any land mammal, and while some whales were bigger than she was, they had the entire ocean to swim around in. Emmy had to bend her head to fit in the garage, as she read a magazine that looked, in her long green talons, no bigger than a matchbook. She looked up at them, her emerald-green eyes moist with sorrow.

"Chad and Amanda are splitsville!" she said in a tragic tone.

"If I were you, I wouldn't believe everything I read in those junky magazines," Daisy said.

"Daisy is right, Emmy. Chad and Amanda are TLFEE," Jesse said.

"What?" Daisy squawked. It was bad enough when Emmy carried on this way, but when Jesse joined in, it was almost more than she could stand.

Jesse explained. "TLFEE. You know, 'true lovers for ever and ever.' Chad and Amanda are America's sweethearts, the Marvelous Two of Malibu. They even go by one name: Chamanda! They're more in love today than they were when romance first sparked on the beach on Maui where they were filming *Blue Rush*."

"Then why is Chad rekindling his old flame, Cindy Curtis, on location in Rome?" Emmy wanted to know.

"Everyone knows they're just good friends," said Jesse. "Besides, Chad's been on the best-dressed list two years running, and Cindy has zero fashion sense. When Joan and Melissa saw her on the red carpet, they said Cindy was a bowwow, not a wow-wow."

"I couldn't agree more," Emmy said. "There was one tier too many of ruffles on that gown of hers. And the color! Puleease!"

"Was that supposed to be pink?" Jesse said. "It looked more like *puke* to me."

"You are so right, Jesse Tiger," Emmy said fervently.

Daisy's small shriek struck them both silent. "Would you two stop talking *tripe*?" she said from between her teeth.

"Sorry," Jesse said sheepishly.

Emmy shrugged. "Actually, tripe can be quite tasty."

Daisy wagged her head. As far as she was concerned, Emmy had become far too wrapped up in the lives of the rich and famous since she had begun reading the movie and gossip magazines from the recycling bin of their neighbor across the street. Because he had grown up so far from the United States, Jesse was more than ready to share this fascination. Luckily, Jesse only talked this way with Emmy, but even that was too much for Daisy.

"How was school today?" Emmy asked sweetly.

Daisy said, "You know how school was. You were there—causing trouble, I might add."

"I wasn't causing trouble," Emmy said. "I was helping. There was a fire, so I fetched the hose."

"It was a fire *drill*," Daisy said.

Emmy looked puzzled. "What is a fire drill?" she asked. "Is it a special tool to drill down through the earth's crust?"

"No. It's when you *pretend* there is a fire so that you can practice getting out of the building in a safe and orderly fashion," Jesse explained patiently.

"Well, in that case, I was *practicing* fetching the hose to put the pretend fire out," Emmy said breezily. "I don't see what the big whoop is. Cool your jets, Daisy Flower. Besides, it gave me a chance to set eyes on that dreamy Dewey Forbes again."

Jesse and Daisy exchanged a look of utter bewilderment: *Dewey Forbes?*

"Dewey Forbes is *not* dreamy," Jesse said.

"Dewey Forbes is a bossy know-it-all," Daisy said.

"Well, maybe I like bossy know-it-alls," Emmy said primly. "Maybe that's why I think Dewey is such a little hottie."

"You know what your problem is, Emmy? You've been reading too much junk," Daisy said as she snatched the magazine from Emmy's talons.

Emmy's eyes took on a cunning gleam. "Well, if you let me go to school with you, maybe I would read *good* things instead."

"No dogs allowed," Daisy reminded her, a little sadly, "and definitely no dragons."

"You just want to be in the same reading group as Dewey Forbes," Jesse teased as he opened his notebook on the picnic table and started his math homework. Dewey was the fastest reader in the class, so fast he had a reading group all to himself. Daisy and Jesse were in the next fastest group, which was fine with both of them. As Uncle Joe always said, "Reading isn't a race; it's an adventure."

"I'm certainly smart enough to be in your class. I can add, subtract, multiply, and do fractions and decimals in my head," said Emmy, peering over Jesse's shoulder. "By the way, Jesse Tiger, the answer to problem number three is twenty-five and a half. Not thirty."

"Don't tell me the answer, Em!" he said. "I'm supposed to figure it out for myself."

"If you get your homework done fast enough, maybe we can go up to the barn and play before dinner," Emmy said eagerly.

Daisy felt a twinge of guilt. It had rained most of last weekend, and they hadn't been up to the barn in almost two weeks. No wonder Emmy was bored. Daisy resolved then and there to try to make quality time for Emmy. Emmy picked up another magazine while the cousins did their homework until Uncle Joe called them in to dinner.

"We're having meat loaf with Krispees, Emmy," Daisy said. "Can I tempt you with leftovers?"

Emmy didn't look up from the pages of *Shimmer, the Magazine for Young Women in the Glow*. "Don't worry about me. I'll just hang out here and calculate my Mating Dating Rating. I'm going to take the quiz and figure out whether I'm 'hot to trot' or 'too cool for school.' I'll nip out later and pick myself up a little something."

"Yeah, a little bunny or a squirrel," Daisy muttered as she and Jesse packed up their books and left the garage.

"I wonder what my Mating Dating Rating is," Jesse wondered aloud.

"Jesse Tiger, stop talking tripe and think! What are we going to do with her? Her head is getting filled up with *junk!*" Daisy said.

"Kids these days," Jesse said with a wag of his shaggy brown head. Daisy punched him on the arm.

"She's fine, Daze, stop worrying," Jesse said, rubbing his arm. "It's just that she has time to burn."

"We'd better get to the library soon and get her some *wholesome* stuff to read," Daisy said.

At dinner, Uncle Joe pounded the bottom of the ketchup bottle over the slab of meat loaf on his plate. "You know, guys, Ms. Goodman is a very nice lady, but I'm not sure I want to be getting phone calls from her every other day."

The cousins sagged against each other.

"We're sorry," said Jesse.

"We're going to try to spend more quality time with Emmy," said Daisy.

Aunt Maggie took the ketchup bottle gently away from her husband and coaxed the ketchup out of the bottle with a butter knife. "I wonder whether we should contact those farmers."

"What farmers?" Jesse asked.

"The farmers whose daughter went away to college," Aunt Maggie said. "You know . . . Emmy's former owners?"

"Oh!" said Jesse. That was a cover story they had made up about how Emmy had come to stay with them. The problem with making up cover stories is that you have to remember them in great detail in case anyone brings them up. Daisy was great at this. Jesse, not so much. He looked to Daisy for an answer.

"They moved someplace far, far away," Daisy said mysteriously.

"Maybe we can find out where they moved—far, far away," Aunt Maggie said, not managing to hide a smile. "I was thinking perhaps they might take Emmy back . . . at least until the school year is over."

Daisy and Jesse both said "NO!" so loudly that Uncle Joe looked up from his meat loaf.

"She's bored, kids. There's nothing for her to do here while you're at school," Uncle Joe said. "And every time we tie her up in the yard, she gets loose and runs off."

"It's really not fair to Emmy to make her stay

16

cooped up in the garage all day long," Aunt Maggie said.

It was a good thing that the phone rang just then, because Jesse and Daisy were fresh out of arguments. The cousins exchanged a helpless look. Of course it was unfair to keep Emmy cooped up in the garage, but what were they supposed to do? She was their dragon and they were her Keepers. There was no giving her away to someone else, even if they wanted to, which they didn't.

They heard Aunt Maggie in the next room talking on the phone. She sounded excited. A few minutes later, she returned to the kitchen, her face flushed and happy.

"Guess what?" she said. "Sherie just gave birth to twins—a boy and a girl!"

"Twins?" Daisy said. "I thought they were just having a girl!"

Sherie was Daisy's brother Aaron's wife. They already had a two-year-old named Paul, Daisy's first nephew and Jesse's first second cousin.

"That's what they thought, too," said Aunt Maggie giddily. "Apparently, the little boy was hiding behind the little girl, so the sonogram didn't pick him up."

"Yeah," said Daisy with a smug look at Jesse, "boys are always hiding behind girls."

"Very funny," said Jesse, kicking Daisy beneath the table.

"I told Aaron we'd fly out and give them a hand. Little Paul's barely out of diapers. I think they're going to need all the help they can get."

"Who's going to look after us?" Daisy said.

"Miss Alodie," said Aunt Maggie.

Jesse and Daisy got up from the table and did their Happy Prospector's Dance. Miss Alodie was their neighbor down the street, a little old garden gnome of a lady who knew that Emmy was a dragon. Having Miss Alodie for a sitter was going to be like having a fairy godmother come over for a slumber party.

The next day at school, Daisy made a card in art class for her new niece and nephew. Jesse made a card for his second cousin Paul, who, he guessed, might be feeling a little left out, not to mention overwhelmed. Throughout the day, Jesse kept looking out the window, expecting to see Emmy out in the schoolyard, romping and clowning around, bringing all the kids over to the window to egg her on the way she often did. But Emmy never showed up. This made Jesse feel both oddly disappointed and very anxious.

He and Daisy were even more disappointed and anxious when they got home after soccer practice to find that Emmy was not waiting for them in the garage. Thinking she might have gone up to the old dairy barn in the meadow behind the house, they went there. But she wasn't in the barn, so they came back and did their homework in the garage, just in case she happened to come home.

At dinner, Uncle Joe and Aunt Maggie kept talking about the new babies, and Jesse and Daisy didn't want to spoil their excitement by mentioning the wayward sheepdog.

"She'll be back by morning" was the last thing Jesse said to Daisy that night before bedtime.

In the morning, when they went out to the garage after breakfast, Emmy still wasn't there. They went back into the house to find that Uncle Joe was on the laptop in the kitchen, getting plane tickets to Boston. Aunt Maggie was leaning over Uncle Joe's shoulder, and they were disagreeing about which box to select next.

"Emmy ran away," Daisy announced.

Uncle Joe's eyes never left the computer screen. "She'll come home when she's ready. She always has before."

"She's never been gone this long," Jesse said. "It's overnight!"

"If she's not home after school today, check the

dog pound," Aunt Maggie said. "It's the blue box, honey. See? It's blinking."

"If all else fails," Uncle Joe said, "you can always put up signs. Isn't that what you guys did when you found that strange lizard that time?"

That strange lizard had been the baby dragon, Emmy, and the signs they had posted had resulted in St. George the Dragon Slayer coming to claim Emmy so that he could drink her blood. Understandably, the cousins were in no hurry to put up any signs this time.

That day at school, they told Ms. Lasky about Emmy running away. Ms. Lasky looked so sad that they thought she might burst into tears. In the afternoon, Ms. Lasky went around the classroom and asked each student what he or she had picked for a science project. Dewey Forbes picked the internal combustion engine. Daisy picked gems and crystals. When Ms. Lasky got to Jesse, he said, "Lost sheepdogs?"

The other kids giggled, but Ms. Lasky smiled gently. "It's not an appropriate topic for a science project, Jesse. But I'll tell you what. Owing to special circumstances, I'm going to give you an extension. Take the long weekend to mull it over."

"Thanks, Ms. Lasky," Jesse said with a grateful sigh.

After school, Jesse and Daisy stopped off at the pound. They searched the cages filled with barking, yapping dogs, but Emmy wasn't there. Ms. Mindy, the dogcatcher, said, "I told you I didn't have any sheepdogs. But don't worry. I'll call if and when Emmy shows."

The cousins continued home in grim silence. Even before they opened the garage door, they could tell Emmy wasn't going to be there: the garage was cold and dark and had a bleak air of abandonment about it. Jesse felt a lump in his throat, and Daisy had the bright-eyed look she got when she was holding tears back. Daisy groped for Jesse's hand, and together they made their way over to the far left corner.

"Whoa!" said Jesse, dropping Daisy's hand.

"Holy moly!" said Daisy.

Emmy's nest was normally overflowing with rolled-up socks. But the socks were gone—every last tube sock, kneesock, and anklet.

"Where did they go?" Jesse asked.

"I have no idea!" said Daisy. Then she said in a determined voice, "But I think it's high time we called in the professor."

21

CHAPTER TWO

TIME TO BURN

Jesse sat down at the computer in his bedroom and keyed in www.foundadragon.org, and the familiar white-bearded face of their online dragon consultant appeared on the screen. He was lighting a pipe. Jesse and Daisy were both a little surprised, because they had never seen him smoking a pipe before. He held up one finger as he puffed away to get the fire started in the pipe's bowl. The cousins waited patiently.

"Ah!" the professor said at last. "Now, what can I do for you two Dragon Keepers today?"

"Emmy ran off," they both said at once, pressing close to the screen.

The professor's bushy white eyebrows rose. "Is . . . that . . . so?" he said, sucking away at his pipe.

"And she took all the socks with her," Daisy added.

"Hmmm," said the professor, frowning. He pulled his pipe out of his mouth and poked a finger around in the bowl.

"He's obviously more interested in his pipe than he is in our problem," Jesse whispered to Daisy.

"Most baffling," said the professor. "No matter how many flames I put to it, the fire in this perfectly well-packed pipe of mine keeps going out."

"What about Emmy?" Daisy blurted out.

The professor leaned back and set down his pipe. "Oh, I shouldn't worry overly much about Emerald. She's older now. Dragons have their own rites of passage, and she was bound to have one sooner or later. Perhaps if I were to try another pipe . . ." The professor got up from his desk chair and wandered out of their view.

The cousins waited a moment, and when he didn't come back, Jesse jabbed his finger at the keyboard and exited the site. "That was not even a *little* bit helpful."

Daisy nudged Jesse. "Look up 'rites of passage,'" she said.

Jesse was already on it. He read aloud from the Wikipedia screen, "'A phrase used to denote rituals marking the transitional phase between childhood and full inclusion into a tribe or social group. Initiation ceremonies range from baptism to bar or bat mitzvahs to tribal scarification.'"

"What's scarification?" Daisy wanted to know.

Jesse, who had lived among African tribes, said, "It's when you scar yourself up to show you're brave and no longer a kid."

Daisy shivered. "I hope she isn't doing anything like that. Maybe her rite of passage is more like a bat mitzvah. You know, with a rented tent and a live band and presents. Do you think she'll invite Dewey?"

"Um, Daisy?" Jesse said. "I'm pretty sure Emmy's not Jewish."

"Oh, right," Daisy said, tearing at her cuticle with her teeth.

Friday morning, Aunt Maggie and Uncle Joe left for the airport just as Jesse and Daisy were setting out for school.

"We'll be back on Tuesday evening," Aunt Maggie said. "I know you're both sad about Emmy, but cheer up. I've never seen a dog more capable of taking care of herself."

At school, Daisy could not keep her mind on her work. She stared out the window and watched the orange and yellow leaves drift down from the maple trees. They gave her an idea.

When it was time to pass out science work sheets, Daisy volunteered to be paper monitor. When she came to Jesse's desk, she leaned in and whispered, "Maybe we should ask the dryads?"

"Definitely!" said Jesse, looking relieved as he took the paper from her.

So after school, Jesse and Daisy ran home and into the backyard, crawled through the tunnel in the laurel bushes, and came out in the pasture by the old dairy barn. On the banks of the brook, there grew a majestic old weeping willow tree, its long fronds trailing in the water. Unlike the other trees, which had burst into rich displays of color, the willow had taken on a sickly yellow cast. Jesse and Daisy stepped across the stones in the brook and ducked beneath the drooping canopy. There he was: his face plainly visible in the gnarled trunk, in the drooping knothole eyes, set just above the jagged line of his mouth.

"Hey, Willow!" Jesse said. "How's it hanging?"

Visiting the willow was like dropping in on a hypochondriac friend. You stood there by his bed, pretending to be interested in his imaginary aches and pains, but all the while you were counting the seconds. They just had to find out what they needed to know and make a clean getaway.

"Don't even ask!" Willow wailed with a rattle of his fronds. "I don't know how I can bear it year after year. Everyone standing around in their autumnal finery and me looking like the wrath of Pan. Go on. Say it. I look like I have a raving case of arboreal jaundice, don't I?"

"You look just fine to me," Daisy said, baring her teeth in a false smile. "Listen, Willow, Jesse and I were wondering if you've seen Emmy lately."

Willow's leaves rustled thoughtfully. "Let me see. Oh, yes, I saw her a few days ago. Looking for someone to play with. Don't ask why she came to me. No one ever asks me to play. Why should they? It's not as if I'm any fun even on a bright summer's day, much less a cold gray one in autumn."

"That's not true," Jesse said. "We used to play with you when we were little. Remember? You were the castle, we were the knights, and the brook was the moat. We had plenty of fun, didn't we, Daze?"

"Sure we did," said Daisy without enthusiasm.

"Did you really?" Willow said, hope boosting the canopy an inch or so. "Oh, that makes me feel so much better! In fact, I may break down and weep for joy."

"Please don't," Daisy said quickly. "Why don't you just tell us about Emmy?"

"Emmy, of course!" Willow said. "Emmy is the princess of the world and I, of course, am but a humble courtier. I told her I couldn't play. Color change is hard work . . . for all of us. After that, we're not good for much of anything but a long winter's sleep."

Jesse prodded the willow. "So, did you have any advice for Emmy?" he asked.

"I told her to run along and play with the hobgoblins. Everyone knows the hobgoblins have time to burn," said the willow, twitching his fronds.

"That's *exactly* what Jesse said about Emmy," Daisy murmured with a thoughtful frown.

"Thanks, Willow!" Jesse said, starting to back away.

"Yeah," Daisy said, "and have fun on your winter's nap."

Willow snorted. "There she goes again with that word. *Fun!* As if being a weeping willow were a romp in the glade!"

Leaving the willow muttering to himself, the cousins swatted their way through the curtain of sallow fronds and got away as fast as they could.

"At least now we've got some fresh clues," Daisy said.

As they made their way down the path into the Deep Woods, all around them they heard the breeze sifting through the branches of the trees. The trees wished them well and confirmed Willow's words. "Shhheee did, she did, she did pass this waaay!" they whispered.

The cousins came to a clearing in the woods and walked to the middle of it, where there was a deep hole with a wide wooden ramp leading to an underground cavern. Two hobgoblins met Jesse and Daisy at the bottom of the ramp, as if they had been expecting them. One held a torch and the other wore the faded purple bandanna Daisy had given him last summer. They stared at the cousins with eyes that were without pupils or irises, red-rimmed and milky white.

"Hello, Hub. Hey, Hermander," Jesse said, no

longer intimidated by these fellows. They looked a little scary but he knew they were really very sweet. "We'd like an audience with Her Royal Lowness."

The hobgoblins' heads bobbed, and they made a dark, moist grunting and snuffling sound through their smashed snouts, a *very underground* sound that Jesse knew was typical of hobgoblins. Then Hub and Hermander turned and headed across the cavern, which rose above them like a vast and stately cathedral made of dirt and tree roots and rock. On the far side, seated upon a mossy throne decorated with tiny snail shells and black pearls, was Queen Hap of the Hobgoblin Hive of Hobhorn, Her Royal Lowness herself. Clad in the shimmering brown finery that flattered her dark-red hair and greenish skin, she was whittling a stick with a sharp, gem-studded knife.

The cousins did what they knew they had to do. They got down on their hands and knees and touched their foreheads to the earth. As they raised their heads, the queen regarded them with regal serenity through moss-green eyes that never blinked.

"Greetings, Keepers!" she boomed in her deep bullfrog voice.

"Greetings, Your Royal Lowness," Daisy said. "We have come because we've lost our dragon.

Willow told us he sent Emmy down here to play with the hobgoblins. Is she still here, by any chance?"

The queen shook her head. "Your draggy-wagon isn't underground with us at present," she said. "But she was here, a day or two ago. She was lonesome and boredsome and wanted to play a game of horsieshoes, but the iron in the horsieshoes hurt her dragon tally-walons. So we took pity on her and made her a safe game to play. We carved the stake ourselves, and some of our loyal subjects wove her ringlets to toss from the bendy-wendy roots of the willow tree. Last we saw her, she was scampering up the ramping, eager to set up her new gamey-wamey and amuse herself with it."

"Thank you, Your Royal Lowness," the cousins said happily as they climbed to their feet.

"Be careful and wareful, Keepers," she said to them, just as they were backing, ever so respectfully, out of her sight.

The cousins froze.

"How careful?" Jesse asked.

"Wareful of what?" Daisy added.

"We hear rumblings and tumblings here under the ground. If we're not mistaken—and we rarely are—things may very well be heating up again," she said, her voice dropping even deeper.

The cousins nodded uncertainly, thanked the queen, and walked back up the wooden ramp.

"What in Sam Hill was Her Lowness talking about?" Jesse asked Daisy as they made their way back through the Deep Woods toward the barn.

"No idea," said Daisy. "St. George is still stuck in that block of amber, so what could she possibly mean by 'heating up'?"

"Not to mention rumblings and tumblings," Jesse added.

When they got back to the barn, they walked around it once, very slowly. Sure enough, on the Deep Woods side of the barn, near an old tree stump, Emmy had driven a carved wooden stake into the ground and set herself up a ringtoss court. The rings woven from the "bendy-wendy" roots of willows were piled neatly at the base of the tree stump. Wrapped around the wooden stake was an old, rusty horseshoe.

Jesse held up the horseshoe. It wasn't just any horseshoe. It was one of the horseshoes from his and Daisy's Museum of Magic. There were three others just like it. They had always imagined that the four shoes had once shod a horse called Old Bub who belonged to the Magical Dairyman. (The Magical Dairyman was their name for the farmer who had once used the barn, a farmer who had turned out to be the professor in a former life.)

"How did Old Bub's horseshoe wind up out here?" Daisy asked. "Emmy can't touch iron."

"Good question," Jesse asked. "But we'd better take it back to the collection. It doesn't belong out here."

Jesse picked up the heavy horseshoe and followed Daisy around to the front of the barn, where she put her back up against the sliding barn door and shoved it open. Inside, the barn was cold and dark and smelled of ancient hay. They made a beeline for the makeshift table—weathered planks laid across sawhorses—that held their Museum of Magic collection.

If you didn't know any better, you would think it was just a bunch of old junk: an ancient three-legged milking stool, some rusty horseshoes, antique hinges, animal skulls, pressed flowers, pinecones, and an old metal ball the size of a peach that the cousins called the Sorcerer's Sphere. The Sorcerer's Sphere gave Jesse an idea.

"Maybe we should drop by the Scriptorium," he suggested. The Scriptorium was a library magically hidden inside the Goldmine City Public Library. In the Scriptorium, each and every one of the books had been a full-fledged dragon at one time. When dragons died, that was where they came to roost. Among the books in the Scriptorium was Emmy's own mother, Leandra of Tourmaline.

"If Leandra doesn't know where Emmy went," Jesse said, "she at least deserves to know that her daughter's gone missing. Plan?"

"Plan!" said Daisy. "Why didn't I think of that? Don't forget the sphere."

Jesse snatched up the sphere, jostling the Toilet Glass, the most recent addition to their collection. It was a medieval compact that imprisoned Sadra the Witch of Uffington.

"Easy does it, J.T.," Daisy said jokingly as Jesse dropped the sphere into the pack on her back. "You wouldn't want to knock the nasty old witch out of her little jailey-wailey, now would you?"

Jesse chuckled because he knew it would take more than a little nudge to break the powerful spell holding the witch prisoner inside the compact.

Jesse and Daisy ran home and hopped on their bikes. They zoomed past Miss Alodie's cottage, the chilly air making their cheeks sting. Miss Alodie was out in her garden wearing a green quilted jacket and a little beanie that looked like the top of a zucchini.

"Hail, cousins!" she called out to them. They slowed down and coasted up onto the sidewalk, bringing their bikes to a standstill. "My carpetbag is all packed, and I'll be over to your house as soon as I've finished mulching," she said cheerily. "Where are you off to in such a tearing rush?"

"Emmy is missing," Jesse said. "And we're going down to the Scriptorium to see if Leandra knows where she might have gone."

"A sensible course of action," she said, bobbing her head. "I'd go with you myself—browsing the Scriptorium is my idea of heaven!—but my flowers need to be tucked in before the first frost nips at their toes. Good luck, cousins!" She picked up her pitchfork and dug into the wheelbarrow full of mulch.

"See you later, Miss Alodie!" Daisy called out as, with the Sorcerer's Sphere bumping around inside the pack on her back, she followed Jesse down the street toward town.

Mrs. Thackeray was sitting at the front desk of the Goldmine City Public Library. She had a gray poodle haircut and was wearing a purple sweatshirt with the words "Library Goddess" spelled out in gold sequins.

The cousins stood before her desk, breathless and flushed from their ride.

"Hi, Library Goddess!" Jesse said with a wave of his hand and a shy grin.

"Hello, you two eager readers! What can I do

for you today?" Miss Thackeray asked.

Daisy was ready with their story, which, as it happened, was the best kind: the truth, in a manner of speaking. "We're doing science projects. I'm doing precious gems, and, um, well, Jesse hasn't figured his out yet, so we thought we'd do a little browsing in the grown-up nonfiction section, if you don't mind."

"Not one bit," said Mrs. Thackeray. "And lucky for you, present company excepted, there are no pesky grown-ups to get in the way of your browsing."

It was true. What was more, there were no pesky kids, either. Daisy and Jesse were the only visitors in the library at the moment, which was a good thing, considering the nature of their real business here.

"You kids browse away. I'll be in the back room unpacking a box of new books. Holler when you need me . . . *in your library voices,* of course!" Mrs. Thackeray added with a wink.

Jesse and Daisy walked over to the grown-up section and headed down the last aisle in the nonfiction section, R to Z. There, at the very end of the aisle, on the floor near the wall, was the miniature manhole. Jesse let out a gasp when he saw that its cover was already open. Working quickly, he unfastened the top of the pack on Daisy's back and peered down into it. The Sorcerer's Sphere lay at the bottom, beginning to glow.

"Okay," said Daisy. "Let's kneel down and lean over the manhole, like we did the last time."

As they did this, Jesse glanced over at their backpack. It was wiggling, like there was something alive inside it trying to get out. The next moment, the Sorcerer's Sphere rolled out of the top of the backpack and down Daisy's arm and disappeared into the mini-manhole with a hollow pop.

The cousins pulled back and shielded their eyes from the blinding white light that came pouring out of the hole. The next minute, the stone floor beneath them gave way, like an elevator in free fall, taking them down with it. Faster and faster they fell, the cool air whistling past their ears. They squeezed their eyes shut and waited for a gentle landing.

Moments later, it came. Just as it had the last time they were here, the sphere stood before them in a holder like a giant golden golf tee. The rusty sphere was now a multifaceted ruby the size of an apple.

The air was foggy, amber-colored, and filled with the aroma of spicy incense. Aisle after aisle stretched out before them, lined with bookshelves rising to dizzying heights and jam-packed with massive books bound in a rainbow of leathers.

"Back in Dragon Heaven," Daisy said.

Overhead, creatures slid from shelf to shelf on a webwork of fine silken filaments, like mountaineers rappelling down a rock face. The shelf elves had unnaturally long arms and legs. Muttering and humming to themselves and to each other, they dusted, adjusted, and fussed over the hundreds upon thousands of dragon volumes.

One of the elves broke away and hurtled downward, landing before them with a crunching sound and a breathless little "Oof!" and a bow. "Oh, there go the knees again! My *word*!"

Willum Wink, Chief Steward of the Shelf Elves of the Scriptorium, stood before them, his brown-checked jacket cinched at the waist with a tool belt. Jesse had forgotten how sharp the shelf elf's features were—the bones of his skull, the nose that hooked down and the chin that hooked up, the jutting cheekbones, the pointy ears, and the piercing eyes that turned up at the corners—topped off with a tuft of hair the color of dust bunnies.

Willum bowed low and said, "Welcome to the Scriptorium!" in a high-pitched warble that sounded like he had been sucking helium from a balloon. "Oh!" he said, with a blink of his eyes. "It's you: the Keepers of the extraordinary Emerald of Leandra. How may I be of service?"

"The extraordinary Emerald of Leandra is missing," Daisy told him. "We've come to tell her mother."

"Our precocious miss is missing, you say?" His eyes crossed over his beaky nose. "(These young people! Never give us a moment's peace, do they now? They most assuredly do not!) You've done well to come here, Keepers. A mother is entitled to know matters of such grave import as this."

Willum Wink gathered up a silken lasso from his tool belt and tossed it high into the foggy golden reaches of the library. The line went taut and then the elf began to pull something heavy, arm over arm. Soon a giant red book with a metal ring on the cover like a door knocker landed on the floor with a dusty *thump*.

Willum Wink cupped his hand over his mouth and called out: "Oh, Leandra! Leandra of Tourmaline! Company's here!"

The heavy cover of the book lifted slowly, the pages fanning as red smoke poured forth, materializing into the giant, ghostly figure of a dragon. From a great height, she stared down with glowing red eyes, red steam pouring from her flared nostrils.

"Emmy is missing," Daisy reported in a voice that trembled only slightly.

"Misssing?" the red dragon hissed. "Misssing *what*? An eye, an ear, a tail, a ssscale, a tongue? Sssurely sshe is perfectly capable of partial sspontaneous regeneration, any daughter of mine!"

Jesse and Daisy exchanged a look. Emmy's mother sounded exceptionally hissy today.

"She's missing *from the garage*," Jesse said. "*All* of her."

The dragon blinked her glowing red eyes.

"Along with all the socks from her nest," Daisy added.

"Ah, yessssss!" said Leandra, her head weaving on her long, sinuous neck. "Ssockss misssing, you sssay? Her current nessst mussst no longer be adequate for her needsss."

Jesse said in a humble voice, "We were going to fix it up and make it bigger this weekend."

Daisy nodded. "We really were going to make improvements. Do you know where she might have gone?"

"Isssn't it obviousss? She hasss gone in sssearch of a new nessst. Her Keepersss, it ssseemsss, have been sssadly remisssssssss!" the dragon hissed as she dissolved into a cloud of red smoke. The smoke pulled back into the pages, and the book slammed shut in their faces.

CHAPTER THREE

HEADING FOR HOT WATER

Jesse, swatting at the smoke, said, "I get the feeling she isn't too happy with us."

Daisy wiped her watering eyes on her sleeve.

"Come on," said Jesse, looking warily about at the hundreds of thousands of volumes of retired dragons sitting on the shelves. "Time to go."

Willum Wink seemed to have returned to his duties, so they went back to where the ruby sphere sat on its giant golf tee. Daisy reached up and grabbed the orb.

Jesse craned his neck and stared upward. The center of the dome, where the Scriptorium exit was, was lost in the swirling mists above them. "How are we supposed to get out of here?" he wondered aloud, feeling a little dizzy. The last time, Emmy had flown them out.

Just then, Jesse felt a breeze riffle the hair on his forehead. The big red book came scooting down the aisle toward them like a magic carpet.

"Don't look now, Jess, but I think our ride is here," said Daisy.

"I guess she couldn't be *too* mad at us, after all," said Jesse.

The cousins scrambled on top of the book and held on tight to the ring as Leandra, in book form, whisked them up through the layers of golden fog, to the tippy-top of the dome. There Daisy popped the sphere into the exit hole. After a few uncomfortable moments of feeling as if they were being squeezed out of a toothpaste tube, they arrived back in the last aisle of the nonfiction section of the Goldmine City Public Library. They clambered quickly to their feet and dusted themselves off.

Daisy found herself nose to nose with a book on crystals and gems. "Well, what do you know?" She took the book down from the shelf and paged through it. "And it has awesome color plates."

They took Daisy's book to the front desk, where Mrs. Thackeray was still on duty. When she saw them, her eyes popped behind her rhinestone spectacles. "My goodness! The two of you look as if you've been dunked in glitter!"

Daisy laughed uneasily and handed her book to the librarian. She stole a glance at Jesse. He did, now that she took the trouble to notice, look as if he were glowing all over. She checked out her own hands and saw that they, too, shimmered as if she had dunked them into a bucket of mica.

They said so long and thanks to Mrs. Thackeray, and then they rode back home. After parking their bikes in the garage—cold and dank and dragonless as it was—they trooped up the back steps, through the mudroom, and into the kitchen. The sight of Miss Alodie standing at the stove, in place of Aunt Maggie or Uncle Joe, caught them both off guard.

In a long, flowered apron, Miss Alodie turned and lifted a wooden spoon in salute. "Heigh-ho, cousins!"

Jesse wrinkled his nose. The kitchen smelled highly unusual, which, he supposed, was to be expected.

"You're just in time for dinner!" Miss Alodie said. Then she got a good look at them and set her wooden spoon down on the stove with a *thunk*. "Land sakes, cousins! You've been *dipped*!"

"In *what*, is the question," said Daisy uneasily.

"Why, in dragon dust!" Miss Alodie said. "What else?"

"I guess you could say that Leandra smoked us by accident," Jesse explained.

Miss Alodie shook her head slowly and firmly. "Keepers, I know accidents when I see them, and this was no accident."

"Anyway," Daisy said, "we're going up to the barn to return the Sorcerer's Sphere to the collection. Then we'll be right back to discuss our findings over dinner."

"Do we have to?" Jesse whispered to her on their way out the door. "Eat dinner, I mean."

"One moment, cousins!" Miss Alodie said. She was rummaging around in a floral-patterned carpetbag. "I have something in here for you." She emerged with a flat, round canteen and handed it to Jesse. It was covered in what looked like purple dragon skin.

43

"What is it?" he asked.

"Keepers, it's clear to me you're headed for hot water," Miss Alodie said, her blue eyes steely. "This will come in handy."

"Thanks, Miss Alodie," said Jesse doubtfully.

Daisy turned around so that Jesse could slip the canteen into the backpack. The weird things Miss Alodie gave them always wound up being very useful.

"We'll be back soon," Daisy said to Miss Alodie as they headed for the back steps.

"Oh, I doubt that very much!" the little old woman called after them. "But don't worry. I'll see you when I see you."

When they got to the barn, Jesse took the sphere out of the backpack. It was once more a crusty old orb. Daisy watched to make sure he returned it to its place on top of the Toilet Glass. That was when she realized that something was again amiss.

"Hey, Jess," she said. "What's wrong with this table?"

Jesse stood back and scanned the objects on the table. His voice rose in alarm. "The horseshoes! *Where are the horseshoes?*"

Not just one but all four of the rusty horseshoes were now missing.

"Let's check outside," Daisy suggested.

They ran outside to where Emmy had set up the ringtoss game behind the barn. Sure enough, the four horseshoes were lying on the ground, two of them near the stake and the other two near the throwing line, all neatly arranged and facing in an easterly direction, as if they were on the feet of a giant, invisible horse.

Jesse knelt to pick up the nearest horseshoe, and when he did, a long brown hind leg appeared, then a switching tail, followed by a sleek, chestnut-colored haunch. Jesse straightened and stepped back. Soon the rest of the animal was visible: a big brown farm horse stood before them with its feet firmly planted in the horseshoes.

"It's Old Bub!" Daisy said, enchanted. "Just how I always imagined him, Jess!"

Old Bub flicked his long tail and plodded over to the tree stump. He stood there for a few moments, his tail swishing back and forth. Then he snorted and scraped the ground with his front hoof, twisting his head around and looking at them with one wise brown eye.

"Um, Daisy?" Jesse said. "I think he wants us to mount and ride."

Jesse boosted himself up onto the tree stump. The horse had no saddle, no stirrups, no halter, and no reins. Jesse grabbed a fistful of wiry mane and hoisted himself up onto Old Bub's swayback. Once settled, with one hand still twisted in the mane, he lowered an arm for Daisy, who had scrambled up onto the tree stump after him. She grabbed hold of his hand, swung herself up behind her cousin, and locked her hands around his middle.

The horse lurched forward, joints creaking and head bobbing.

"Whoa!" said Jesse.

The horse shuddered to a halt.

"What's happening?" Jesse said.

"You just said, 'Whoa,' Jess," Daisy pointed out, with a nervous giggle.

"I didn't mean it *that* way," Jesse said. "I meant it like 'Woweee!'"

"Yeah, well, Old Bub doesn't know the difference, do you, old feller? Let's try this." Daisy squeezed Old Bub's rib cage with her legs and said, "Giddyup!"

Old Bub started up again. Daisy let out a sigh of relief. Considering that the horse was so huge, it was nice to know they had a *little* control over him. Daisy had ridden horses before, but not many as large as this one, and none, of course, that were magical!

The horse was heading in an easterly direction down the winding barn road. Daisy, peering out from behind Jesse, saw something lying ahead of them on the road. It was a small, white object.

"What's that?" she said, pointing.

As they came closer, she saw that it was a rolled-up pair of clean white tube socks.

"Socks . . . from Emmy's nest!" Jesse said. "Should we stop and pick them up?"

Daisy shook her head. "No, we'll pick them up later. If we get down now, we'll never be able to get back on again. Let's just find out where he's taking us."

The horse plodded on down the barn road and crossed the street. His heavy hooves clip-clopped loudly on the pavement, then became muffled again as he entered the woods on the far side. The cousins had never been in these woods before. Tall pine trees grew so close together that they blocked out the sun, tinged the air deep green, and filled it with the smell of Christmas. It wasn't long before they passed a ball of bright-red kneesocks.

Daisy said, "Wasn't *Hansel and Gretel* one of Emmy's favorite books when she was little?"

"Only after she got over being terrified of the witch in the woods and the kids in the cage, yeah," Jesse said.

"So are you thinking what I'm thinking?" said Daisy.

Jesse was silent for a bit. "You think Emmy's left a trail for us?" he asked.

"Socks instead of stones or bread crumbs," Daisy said, her heart quickening. "Let's hope."

As if Old Bub sensed her excitement, he switched to a trot. Daisy gripped Jesse, and Jesse gripped the horse's mane. Just as they were getting used to having their teeth rattling around in their heads, the horse lengthened his stride into a smooth canter.

"Woweeeee!" Jesse said.

Old Bub rolled up an old logging trail filled with ruts, which he rocked over with heart-stopping ease. The socks kept coming—dark blue, hot pink, Argyle, striped, polka-dotted—one after the other, as Old Bub flattened his gait into a gallop.

Daisy's stomach lurched and her nose ran, but she didn't dare let go of Jesse to wipe it. Daisy had been on a galloping horse for one or two breath-taking sprints, but this was a run that went on for so long that it wasn't possible to keep holding her breath. She was soon exhausted and panting, as if it were she and not the horse who was doing the running. And all the while, there was the steady *creak-creak-creak* of the horseshoes, like rusty hinges opening the door to . . . *who knew what?*

Suddenly, they plunged into deep shadow. Daisy looked up and gasped. Over the jagged tree-tops, the snowcapped mountain loomed, shockingly close and glowing pale pink in the rays of the lowering sun.

"Yep!" Jesse said, as if his suspicion was now confirmed. "That's where we're headed. High Peak!"

"Emmy's first nest," Daisy said, and a shiver of anticipation rippled through her.

The path grew steeper, and now the sock balls became single socks, stretched out like bright arrows pointing the way upward in the gathering gloom. The route they were on was familiar from hikes they had taken with Uncle Joe. Old Bub leaped up the steep paths with the nimbleness of a mountain goat.

Jesse lay along Old Bub's neck, arms grimly tangled in the mane. Daisy clung to Jesse, her cheek pressed to his back. Beneath her interwoven fingers, she felt the wild beating of Jesse's heart. Daisy was sure her own heart was beating just as rapidly. What had been exciting was now terrifying. What if the horse's hooves slipped on the rocks?

What if the two of them slid off his back? Would they tumble backward off the side of the mountain?

After a long while, the terrain began to level off a bit and the horse slowed to a trot. The wind pounded Daisy's back like icy fists and made her glad for her winter coat. She opened her eyes and looked around. The trees had dwindled to almost nothing. They were on the upper slopes of High Peak, above the timberline. It was a good twenty degrees colder up here. The wind whipped their hair every which way and worked its frigid fingers down the collars of their coats.

Jesse untangled his right hand from Old Bub's mane long enough to point to a group of boulders lying up ahead. This was the spot where Jesse had found the geode from which Emmy had hatched. But Old Bub lurched right past the spot and crunched up the snowy hillside toward the summit.

At the top of High Peak, there was a lake, no bigger than the pool of a large public fountain but much, much deeper. Uncle Joe always said that it was deeper than the highest skyscraper was high, because it was the water-filled crater of an extinct volcano whose core reached down to the magma layer beneath the earth's crust.

Old Bub stopped on the banks of the lake and, reminding Jesse of a bus that had come to the end of the line, released a long puff of steam and settled his body to say he was done.

The cousins gratefully slipped down from Old Bub's back. The horse wandered off and dropped his head to nibble at the blades of dull-green dried grass poking up through the snow. Jesse and Daisy staggered around, catching their breath, shaking out their limbs, and checking themselves for bruises.

Jesse stopped suddenly and looked at the lake. It was a body of water so freezing cold that nobody ever swam in it, even after a vigorous climb on the hottest day of the summer. In the last rays of the setting sun, wisps of steam rose off its glassy surface.

Daisy knelt, dipped a hand in the water, and quickly pulled it out. "It's boiling hot, Jess."

The cousins stared down into the water's crystalline depths.

"And look!" Daisy said, pointing. "See it? There's another sock . . . under the water." Shivering, Daisy straightened and stepped back.

Jesse went behind Daisy and unfastened the backpack. Daisy watched as he came around and unscrewed the top of the purple canteen. Throwing back his head, he took a healthy swig from it. At first, his face puckered up something fierce. Then

51

his eyes popped open, his mouth gaped, and he began to pant.

"Jesse Tiger, what in Sam Hill are you *doing*?" Daisy asked, worried. "Are you choking? Can you speak?"

"What Miss Alodie said to do," he said between gasps. "This stuff is for when we run into hot water, which is exactly what we just did." He gestured at the steaming lake.

"I get it!" Daisy grabbed the canteen. She closed her eyes and gulped. She shuddered from head to toe. It tasted minty cold. At first, it gave her such bad brain freeze she thought her eyes would pop out of her head, but then it rapidly turned piping hot. She opened her mouth to let the steam out. "What is in that stuff?" she said, wiping her mouth on her coat sleeve and handing the canteen back to Jesse.

Jesse shrugged. "With Miss Alodie, you never know," he said. Screwing the cap back on, he returned the canteen to the backpack. "I only know that we have to keep following the path or we'll never find our dragon."

"You mean into the hot water?" Daisy said slowly, her blue eyes wide.

Jesse nodded. "If that's what it takes."

Jesse was always the last in the water when it

was cold, so it shouldn't have been much of a surprise to Daisy that he would be the first into hot water. Still, she was astonished to see him step so casually into the lake and walk toward the submerged sock. The water came quickly up to his waist.

"Jesse Tiger . . . ," Daisy said in a warning voice.

"I see another sock after this one," Jesse said. "I'm just going to try and get to it."

She watched as the water came up to his neck and then as his shaggy head disappeared beneath the surface.

"Jesse!" she screamed.

The water felt as warm and soothing as bathwater. "Wait till you try this, Daze!" he said, but a trail of bubbles glugged lazily out of his mouth instead of his voice. This was like no water he had ever been in. For one thing, he could breathe in it! For another thing, his body didn't bob up to the surface. His body felt heavy and comfortable. This was so much more enjoyable than getting jounced around in the freezing cold on the back of an old farm horse.

Moving slowly underwater, Jesse turned around and looked at Daisy. She was running back and forth on the shore and hollering. Her voice sounded far away. He raised his hand and beckoned to her.

She flung up her arms and waded in after him. Then he heard the first exclamation of wonder as her body met the water. By the time she was under the water with him, she wore a silly grin on her face.

Jesse turned and made his way toward the next sock . . . and the next. They were all white gym socks, lying on the ever steeper gradient of the lake bottom. He slid down, Daisy tumbling after him. Soon they were slipping and sliding down a soft muddy slope, one sock after another passing them, faster and faster, like a painted dotted line on a highway at night, until all Jesse saw as he fell was one long, continuous white line trailing past him as the lake got deeper and darker and steeper. He wondered how long it would take them to reach the pool of molten lava beneath the earth's crust.

Jesse figured that he must have fallen asleep, because he woke up with a start, his body smooshed up against a warm stone wall. Daisy gently collided into his back. He pushed himself away from the wall. Tapping his shoulder, Daisy pointed to a long jagged crack running down the face of the rock wall. A rich red light shone through a wide spot in it. Into this crack Jesse fitted the fingers of both hands and pulled, as if he were opening a stubborn set of elevator doors.

The crack gradually widened, letting in more of the rich red light. Jesse squinted into it. Eventually, the crack was wide enough to fit his body. He squeezed through, blinking, scarcely able to believe his eyes. He let out a whoop of astonishment, which was when he realized that he could hear his own voice again and was no longer immersed in the warm water.

"What is it?" Daisy poked her head around him to see for herself. "Holy cow!"

"It looks like the Emerald City of Oz!" Jesse said.

"Made of rubies instead of emeralds!" Daisy said. "A Ruby City!"

Before them stood a dazzling scarlet cluster of arches, atriums, and domes, as delicate as blown glass, dominated by a single elegant spire that rose up into a pomegranate red sky and pierced a layer of clouds resembling pink cotton. Red crystal vehicles that looked like giant sleighs, pulled by teams of fire-breathing animals, shuttled up and down wide boulevards lined with trees. The trees had ebony braided trunks, leaves of topaz and emerald, and fruits of garnet and sapphire.

"What *is* this place?" Jesse said as he took a step forward.

Daisy hauled him back by the belt. When he

looked down, his stomach lurched. It was at least a hundred-foot drop to another lake, larger than the one they had just fallen through and holding in its limpid surface the reflection of the magnificent city on its far shore. Daisy squeezed in beside him just as the crack in the rock closed behind them, leaving them stranded on a ledge not much wider than a balance beam.

Chapter Four

THE GRAND BEACONS

"What now?" Jesse asked, his voice shrinking. Flying around on Emmy's back had gone a long way toward curing his fear of heights, but he wasn't on Emmy's back now, and he was scared.

Daisy groped around for his hand and said,

"What else can we do? We go jump in the lake."

"No way," said Jesse, shutting his eyes and grinding his back into the stone wall, hoping it would open up and let him back inside.

"Look down, Jess," Daisy said.

"I don't want to look down," Jesse said, squeezing his eyes shut all the more tightly.

"Just *do* it," she prompted him gently. "Trust me."

He opened one eye and looked down.

"What do you see?" Daisy asked softly.

"I see a gym sock floating on the lake," Jesse said, opening the other eye and starting to breathe normally again.

"And that's exactly why," Daisy said, seizing his hand and pulling him with her as she leaped into the air, "we j-u-u-u-u-m-p!"

Feet kicking and arms flailing, Jesse screamed all the way down. His scream was cut short as they sank into the soft surface of the lake. They floated up and then came down and bounced on top several times before they finally sank into the warm and oozy mire.

If the crater lake had been warm maple syrup, this stuff was like hot toffee—or, Jesse thought, *molten lava*. But how could it be? The temperature of hot lava was something like two thousand degrees Fahrenheit. If this were lava, wouldn't they be burned to a crisp? Then he thought he had an answer.

"The dragon dust and the stuff in Miss Alodie's canteen are protecting us," Jesse said, but Daisy was out of earshot. She was swimming, or rather wallowing, across the lake, toward the shore.

"Wait up!" he called out to her.

By the time he joined her, she was running up and down the beach scooping up handfuls of pebbles. Jesse noticed that neither of them was wet, and that their clothing was steaming like a bunch of laundry pulled out of a hot dryer. And yet, in spite of the heat of the place, he didn't feel overheated in his winter clothing. It was very strange.

"Gemstones, Jess!" Daisy held out her hands and showed him rubies, sapphires, topazes, emeralds, as worn and translucent as beach glass, ranging in size from peppercorn to lima bean. She filled her coat pockets with them.

"Isn't that stealing?" Jesse asked uneasily.

"How could it be stealing? The beach is full of them. There are tons and tons of them. Look around you, Jesse! This whole place is made of precious and semiprecious gemstones and crystals. It's *gorgeous!*"

Daisy was right. Now that he got a closer look at the Ruby City, he saw that while rubies were the principal building material, in and among the ruby spires and arches and domes were flashes of sapphire and topaz and amber and maybe even diamond. It was like gazing into a fire. At first, all you saw was red, but when you looked closer, you saw streaks of orange and blue and yellow and white and green.

"I wonder who lives here," he said.

"Dragons!" Daisy crowed as she pointed down the beach. Two very large dragons were bounding toward them. They were tossing a ball that looked as if it were made of fire. As the dragons drew nearer, the smaller one looked very familiar.

"It's Emmy!" he shouted.

"It is! It is!" said Daisy, flapping her hands in excitement.

They both began jumping up and down and calling out to their dragon.

Emmy pulled up short and waved both arms. Tossing the ball to the other dragon, she popped open her wings and skimmed along the beach toward them. "Jesse! Daisy! My favorite Keepers!" she cried, catching them up in her arms.

"We're your *only* Keepers, I hope," said Jesse as he nestled against bright scales that were, if anything, more dazzling here than at home. "We thought we'd lost you."

"But you followed my trail of socks and found me. Aren't I a clever dragon?" Emmy said with a pleased chuckle.

"You're the cleverest dragon in the world!" Daisy said.

"Oh, no!" Emmy said, setting them back down again and shaking her head. "Jasper is the cleverest dragon in the world. He's my fiery mote."

"Your *what*?" Jesse asked.

"The fiery mote of my heart," Emmy said. "That's what they call boyfriends and girlfriends here."

They all watched as the other dragon—the fiery mote of Emmy's heart—approached.

"I thought a mote was a tiny little thing," Daisy whispered to Jesse. "This guy's anything but."

Emmy said shyly, "Jesse and Daisy, meet my fiery mote, Jasper."

Jasper bowed to them. "The adorable child exaggerates," he said in a rumbling voice. "Emerald and I are just boons."

"Boons?" Daisy asked.

"He means friends," Emmy said. "And we're that, too."

Jesse stared up at the hulking dragon. Much

larger than Emmy, he had bronze-gold scales that looked like medieval armor. Jesse felt more than a little intimidated, and it wasn't just the dragon's size. It was the two heavy bronze horns that sprang from his head. Emmy's horns were just little nubs. These horns were long and sharp. What did Emmy see in this guy? He was about as far from Dewey Forbes as you could get!

"How do you do?" Daisy said. "Any boon of Emmy's is a boon of ours."

Daisy prodded Jesse with a sharp elbow.

"It's nice to meet you," Jesse said with a nod. "Nice, uh, *horns* you got there," he added rather awkwardly.

"Aren't they *magisterial*?" Emmy said adoringly.

Jesse thought they made him look like a monster Viking or a king-size devil, but he said, "So, how did you two kids meet?"

"Right here on the shores of the Lake of Fire!" Emmy said. "Isn't it romantic? Like Chad and Amanda in Maui!"

"The Lake of Fire?" Jesse said. "I don't see any fire."

As if on cue, they heard a dull roar. A mound, like a mini-volcano, erupted from the surface of the lake, spewed a fountain of fire and magma, and then subsided.

"What *is* this place?" Daisy asked.

"The Fiery Realm!" Emmy said. "And that there is the Ruby City. Isn't it nifty?"

Jasper bent and rumbled something into Emmy's ear.

"Whispering must not be rude in the Fiery Realm," Daisy commented to Jesse through tightly clenched teeth.

When Jasper was finished whispering, Emmy said to them, "I must take you to meet Lady Flamina and Lord Feldspar."

"Who?" Jesse asked.

"The Grand Beacons of the Fiery Realm," said Emmy. "I have met them many times. Jasper says it's against the Beacons' Code for you to be here without their sanction. Come on."

Jesse and Daisy hurried along after the two dragons as they led the way through a set of soaring arched gates into the heart of the Ruby City.

Jesse said, "I don't know about you, Daze, but I don't trust anyone with horns like that."

Daisy didn't respond. She was too busy taking in the sights. Up close, the sleighlike vehicles were enormous, with tiers of seats rising up like bleachers. They were pulled by teams of hulking pink lizards. The passengers looked like rows of flickering flames. Down the sidewalk, more flames rushed toward them. As the flames drew nearer, Daisy made out jagged humanoid shapes within them, with long legs and long arms, not unlike the shelf elves but with fierce-looking faces framed by flaming tresses.

"What *are* they?" Daisy asked.

"Fire fairies," said Emmy. "They inhabit this realm, along with the dragons and other fire creatures, both wild and tame."

"But I thought fairies had wings," said Jesse.

"Not here," said Emmy. "Fire fairies don't fly. They flit . . . and skip and jump, but they don't fly."

There were dragons, too, sharing the wide promenade, some alone, some accompanied by other dragons, others walking with fire fairies. Like Jasper, all the dragons had prominent horns, quite a few having more than two. Some seemed in a hurry; others took their time, stopping to look in the shop windows that displayed an array of elegant goods: necklaces and bracelets and tiaras, vases and bowls and goblets, shoes and hats and beautiful sparkling gowns. Daisy wanted to linger and browse, but Emmy and Jasper hustled them along until they came to a giant gate hewn from rose quartz.

Two towering fire fairies holding gold lances stood guard on either side of a grand arched entryway carved from ruby. Daisy looked up. Ruby arches soared and disappeared into the pink clouds. This was the palace with the spire she had seen from up on the ledge.

"The Great Hall of the Grand Beacons," Emmy said in a hushed tone.

One of the guards came down the ruby steps to have a word with Jasper. The guard nodded and stood back. The next moment, the gates swung open and Jasper herded them in. They walked up the wide stairs and passed through an arched doorway into a long ruby-red gallery that reminded Daisy of how she imagined the inside of the throat of a long-necked monster might look. It was flanked by more armed guards with lances, who seemed to crackle and sputter as the procession passed.

The gallery opened up into a massive chamber housing what appeared to be a great stone fireplace at the far end. As they came nearer, Daisy realized it was a giant throne that looked like a nest of rubies. Seated upon the throne-nest were a fire fairy and a large dragon with pewter-gray scales and three horns splayed across his huge head.

"Jesse and Daisy, may I present to you the Grand Beacons of the Fiery Realm, Lady Flamina and Lord Feldspar," Emmy said, her voice swelling with pride. "Lord and Lady, these are my Keepers, Jesse Tiger and Daisy Flower. They followed me here from the Earthly Realm."

"The Earthly Realm, is it? Nice to know where we come from," Jesse muttered to Daisy.

"Shhhh!" Daisy said. "Listen."

"Welcome to the Fiery Realm," said Lady Flamina. When she spoke, her face and hair flickered vivid blue. Her voice sounded like fire spitting on damp wood.

The dragon at her side nodded his huge horned head and sighed, wisps of black smoke trailing from his nostrils.

"I was right, was I not?" Lady Flamina said to her dragon companion. "I said I heard them coming and here they are."

"You are correct as usual, Your Ladyship," Lord Feldspar growled.

"That was probably me," Jesse said. "I screamed my head off when Daisy dragged me over the ledge into the Lake of Fire."

The fire fairy flared up bright orange. "No one in the Ruby City missed that. But I heard you coming long before you passed through the membrane. I heard you as you rode across the earthly terrain toward us on your iron-shod steed. You see, we in the Fiery Realm can see anything in the Earthly Realm that is in flames."

Jesse nodded politely.

The fire fairy went on: "I realize this notion may be beyond your feeble Earthly Realm powers of perception, so I won't pursue this any further for fear of making you feel less enlightened than you already do."

"Oh, no!" Jesse said. "I understand. What you're saying is that Old Bub's shoes are rusty iron. Rust, as a corrosive substance brought about by oxidation, is a lesser form of combustion. So you 'heard,' rather than saw, the rust coming toward you, right, Flamina?"

Daisy cocked an eye at Jesse. Sometimes she was amazed at how much her cousin knew. Her father said it was because he was mostly home-schooled by his parents, two very smart doctors.

Her Ladyship, however, seemed more angry than impressed. She flared up into several small, blazing yellow peaks. "That's *Lady* Flamina to you, earthly upstart!"

"*Lady* Flamina," Jesse said, cringing.

The fire fairy sighed and went back to orange and then to pale blue. "The Grand Beacon of Dragons and I have conferred, and we have ruled that you will be allowed to stay here for two Earthly Realm days, which are roughly equivalent to ours. Then you must leave. These are trying times in the Fiery Realm, and we can brook no interlopers."

Daisy opened her mouth to speak, but Jesse beat her to it. "Your Esteemed Royal Lady Beaconship—and Your Lordship, too, of course—we beg you to brook us a full three Earthly Realm days' visit instead of two," he said. "You see, Monday is Teachers' Conference Day. That's when all the teachers get together to talk about teaching methods and stuff and we don't have to go to school, and besides, Daisy's parents are away in Boston with Daisy's big brother, my cousin Aaron, whose wife Sherie just had twins—which would make Daisy an aunt and me a second cousin for the second and third time—and Miss Alodie, the neighbor down the street who is taking care of us, understands that we are Keepers, and she pretty much said that she'd see us when she sees us, so—"

"Desist with the dithering details!" Her Ladyship flared up as if someone had poured oil on her flame. She faced Lord Feldspar. The two exchanged hissing whispers. The fire fairy looked at the cousins at length and said, "Very well, the Beacons have revised their ruling. You may stay for three days or until you have exhausted your supply of Fiery Elixir, whichever comes sooner. After that, you will leave or else die a horrible death."

"We'll leave *and* take our dragon with us," Daisy said, just to be sure everyone knew where they stood.

The top of Her Ladyship's head sharpened to a high, white-hot peak as she whispered: "Never!"

"I beg your pardon?" Daisy said boldly.

Lord Feldspar's voice hit her like the blast from a furnace. "Emerald of Leandra is to remain here! She will stay and take her place in the Fiery Realm. This is the realm she has chosen and this is the realm she will inhabit until it is time for her to merge with the Great Flame!"

Beside him, Jesse sensed Daisy pulling herself up tall. "We are her Keepers, and it is not your place, or hers, to make such life-changing decisions," she said.

Lady Flamina's flame leaped up to twice the size of the massive dragon beside her. The room exploded in white light, out of which Lady Flamina's voice came at them quick and cold and sharp as an ice pick: "Remove your upstart selves from our midst!"

One moment, Emmy and Jasper, Jesse and Daisy were facing the throne. The next minute, they were all standing outside the closed door of the throne room. Their bodies gave off wisps of gray smoke. None of them could say how they had gotten there, but all of them felt as if they had been struck by lightning.

"Let's get out of here," Jesse said in a stunned voice.

Daisy wanted to march back into the throne room and give the Grand Beacons what for, but the others talked her out of it and, reluctantly, she followed them down the hall.

Daisy fumed. "The nerve of those—"

"Easy, Daisy," Jesse said, his eyes on the lines of snarling guards flanking them. "It is their realm, and it won't help Emmy if you get us kicked out for being upstarts."

Jasper and Emmy, engaged in furious whispers, beat a hasty retreat down the long ruby-red gallery toward the exit.

Daisy caught up and elbowed her way between the two dragons. "It's not nice to tell secrets, you two."

"Jasper is saying that you got the Beacons' blood boiling," Emmy said.

Daisy felt pretty hot-blooded herself. "Is Feldspar right, Em? Have you chosen to stay here forever and ever until you merge with the Great Flame . . . whatever the Sam Hill that is?"

Emmy looked down at Daisy and blinked, her emerald eyes clouded with doubt. "I want to be near my fiery mote."

"But, Emmy," Jesse said, "you heard what Lady Flamina said. If you stay here, you'll merge one day with the Great Flame. That means you won't get to join your mother in the Scriptorium."

Emmy looked troubled, as if this idea had not occurred to her until this moment.

"Now, Emerald," Jasper chided her gently, "your rightful place *is* with your Keepers."

Daisy nearly hugged Jasper in gratitude and surprise.

"Listen to the big bronze guy," Jesse said.

"Ah, but our boon has a mind of her own," Jasper said. "I would like to stay with you longer, but I must leave you now." They were standing outside the gates of the palace. "I will see you all here at the Great Hall tomorrow first thing for the royal runching. Good day, Emerald. Good day, Keepers." Jasper bowed his horned head and headed off down the street.

"Do we *have* to come back here?" Jesse asked. "This Great Hall isn't so great, if you ask me. And what's with 'runching'?"

"Oh, but it's a huge honor to be invited to a royal runching," Emmy said, distracted. "I didn't get my good-bye clinch. Excuse me, Keepers." She ran after Jasper.

Jesse and Daisy looked on as Emmy caught up to Jasper and thrust her head to either side of his. It looked sort of like the way people in Europe kiss, first one cheek and then the other, except that it went on longer and no kisses were exchanged. It was just a bunch of head bobbing.

"I guess that must be clinching," Jesse said.

"Whatever it is, our girl sure doesn't believe in playing hard to get," Daisy murmured sadly.

Jesse turned away. "Tell me when the two love-birds are finished with their weird ritual," he said.

Daisy said dolefully, "It's going to take a mighty powerful plan to pull those two apart."

Jesse threw up his arms. "How are we supposed to come up with a decent plan in only three days in this totally hostile environment?"

"I don't know . . . but we're going to have to," Daisy said. "If we want to keep our dragon."

Emmy came back, heaving a huge and sappy sigh. "I miss him already!" she said. "Isn't he dreamy?"

"Dreamier than Dewey Forbes, at least," Jesse said grudgingly.

"He's very nice," said Daisy carefully. "But doesn't he seem a little old for you?"

Emmy shrugged. "Everyone knows older males are so much more worldly and intriguing," she said.

Daisy rolled her eyes.

"It's true!" said Emmy. "I read an article about it in *Shimmer*. 'Mature Males Make Better Mates.'"

"You read that article to me," Jesse put in. "It also said same-age guys make better dates. And you're way too young to get married."

"Silly boy," Emmy said. "Dragons don't get married."

"What *do* dragons do?" Daisy asked.

Emmy thought for a moment and then heaved her shoulders. "Beats me! I'm new to all this. Come on! Let me show you my new home."

"Home?" Daisy echoed shrilly.

Was Leandra right? Had Emmy found herself a new nest?

CHAPTER FIVE

IN THE GLOAMING

They went with Emmy down a diamond-paved road that wended its way along the shoreline of the Lake of Fire.

"It's so dark here," said Jesse. "When does the sun come out and brighten things up?"

"Never," said Emmy. "There is no sun. It's always sort of dark like this. Isn't it cozy?"

Jesse had read about places where, during the winter, it was almost always dark. But in those areas, it was also freezing cold. It felt odd being in a place that was always dark and yet was as hot as equatorial Africa. It looked much the way things did in his dreams: dim and shadowy and a little spooky. He didn't like it. "It's too weird," he said.

"Oh, give it a chance, Jesse Tiger," said Emmy.

On the way to Emmy's house, they passed dragons out strolling who nodded to Emmy as if they had known her always. Two of them stopped to say hello.

"These are my boons, Opal and Galena," Emmy said.

The two she-dragons were bigger than Emmy, one pale and lustrous, the other with lilac-colored scales.

"We're so lucky that little Emmy landed in our midst!" Galena gushed.

Opal added, "Emerald is one of a kind!"

"Are you and Jasper coming to the Fire Ball?" Galena asked.

Emmy suddenly looked bashful. "I don't know . . . he hasn't asked me yet."

"Oh, he will!" said Opal.

Galena said to Opal in a meaningful undertone, "What if *you-know-who* comes back?"

"Emmy can take care of herself," said Opal.

After Opal and Galena had gone on their way, Daisy said, "Who is you-know-who?"

"Who knows?" said Emmy. "It's not like I've met every single solitary fairy and dragon in the realm. Not yet, at least. But I plan to. I like it here so much."

"Just how long have you been coming to this place?" Jesse asked.

"Since you started school," Emmy said. "Each time I visited, I liked it a little more. Then I met Jasper and the dime was cast."

"That would be *die*," Jesse said. "The singular of dice."

"The dice was cast," Emmy said, standing corrected.

"What did Lady Flamina mean by 'trying times'?" Daisy wanted to know.

Emmy's brow furrowed and she leaned down and whispered as if there were spies about. "Some of the smaller fire fairies have been mysteriously disappearing—"

Suddenly, the ruby-berried bushes on their right erupted into flames. Three fire fairies, about a third the size of Jesse and Daisy, popped out and cried: "Emmy-Emmy-Emmy!"

They bounced over and latched onto Emmy's tail, bouncing energetically up and down. "Go! Go! Go! Give us a lift, Emmy!"

Emmy laughed and walked on, giving the three little fire fairies a ride on her tail. "Jesse and Daisy, these are my boons Spark, Flicker, and Fiero," Emmy said, pointing to each of them in turn.

Spark had a head that came to an orange point like the flame on a birthday candle. Flicker flickered, white one moment and blue the next. Fiero was smaller than the other two and round.

"Spark and Flicker are boys. Fiero's a girl," Emmy pointed out.

"You're Emmy's Keepers, aren't you?" Fiero said, growing even rounder and rosier-looking when she spoke.

"Emmy's told us all about you," Spark said.

"Can you be *our* Keepers, too?" Flicker asked, his voice as tentative as his flame. "And protect us from the fairy-nappers?"

"Feeble-flamer!" Spark scoffed. "There are no Keepers in this realm. Why do you think they can't stay?"

"They can stay if they like," Fiero said smugly. "Because Keepers have special powers."

"What special powers?" Spark said.

"The powers conferred upon them by the purple flask of the fire serpent," Fiero said.

"How did you know about that?" Jesse asked.

Fiero shrank into a bashful little ball. "I licked up through the crater lake and saw you standing on its banks, swigging from the purple flask."

"Fiero!" Spark shrilled. "No fair! Why didn't you take us with you when you did that?"

"Maybe because it's against the Beacons' Code to lick into the membrane," Flicker said.

"Oooh, that's true!" Spark scolded Fiero. "Bad, bad flame!"

"At least I'm bolder than you two pale embers," Fiero scoffed. Then, turning to Jesse and Daisy, she said, "Emmy is our favorite dragon. She's much more fun than the others. She likes to *play*."

"Don't dragons play in the Fiery Realm?" Daisy asked.

Emmy said, "They can play but they can't fly. I'm the only one who can fly, although I am not supposed to fly here. But the dragons here can do something I can't. They can flame. You should see them. They have contests to see who can hurl the biggest flame."

"What fun," Daisy said politely, but it sounded dangerous to her.

"Does anyone know who's napping the fire fairies?" Jesse asked.

Flicker whispered, "Some say they just get extinguished by strange forces. Others say they have been spirited away to other realms!"

"That's why we tag around after Emmy," said Spark.

"Emmy will protect us," said Fiero.

"Then she's like *your* Keeper," Daisy said.

"Yay! Emmy's our Keeper!" Fiero said, bouncing around like a little rubber ball.

"Here we are at my cozy cottage, cousins!" Emmy said at last.

Jesse and Daisy stared up at it.

Emmy's "cottage" looked remarkably like Miss Alodie's house, only about three times as large and with a wide porch overlooking the Lake of Fire. It was made of fat, shiny lozenges of precious stone held together with mortar. The mortar was molten and throbbed like a living thing. There was even a garden, planted with rows of ruby and amethyst dahlias and long-stalked sunflowers with drooping topaz heads.

"I love your garden!" Daisy said.

"We helped Emmy make it," Spark said. "But we have to leap along now. We'll catch up with you later!"

"At the royal runching!" Flicker added, as the three of them flitted off down the path.

"I like them," Jesse said. The idea that anyone would want to kidnap such cute little creatures made him seethe with anger.

"I like them, too," Emmy said as she led the cousins up a set of amethyst steps and through the front door. "And looky-looky. My head doesn't bump the ceiling!" Emmy jumped up and down to demonstrate. "Now do you see why I like this place? I have my very own home with a living room and a couch and a bedroom and a generous porch. There's no nosy neighbors, and the best part is I don't have to be a sheepdog ever!"

Daisy slid her eyes toward Jesse. Jesse sighed. They had both known Emmy was bored with being their pet sheepdog, but they hadn't realized until this moment just how fed up she was.

Emmy went on enthusiastically, "And if I want to make my house bigger, I just do this."

The cousins watched as she touched one of the walls and began to mold the mortar as if it were clay. As she pushed outward, the mortar stretched, and the precious stones multiplied. Before the cousins' astonished eyes, Emmy added a brand-new room to her cottage. "See? Now I have made you two your very own bedroom!"

Jesse and Daisy watched as she went on to furnish the room, forming two beds side by side, with lava mattresses and blankets and pillows. There was even a table between the beds that held a computer. It was an almost exact replica of Jesse's room, right down to the rug on the floor and the fancy computer keyboard sitting on the desk.

"Is that a working computer?" Daisy asked, giving Jesse a meaningful look that he knew meant *Maybe we can contact the professor and find out how to get Emmy out of this place.*

"Oh, no," Emmy said. "But I thought it would make you feel more at home. Let me show you my room."

Emmy took them next door, where there was a familiar-looking packing crate, twice as big as the one in the Earthly Realm. The slats were made of amber, and it was filled with lava socks. "Look, cousins! It's just like my nest at home, only the right size, and I'm next door to you, in case you wake up in the middle of the night and need me."

Wait a minute, Daisy wanted to say, *aren't we the Keepers?* But she didn't, because Emmy was totally caught up in the task of folding up pads of lava and adding more socks to the mound in her crate. The sight of Emmy making herself so at home in this strange place made Daisy want to weep.

Emmy stood back and admired her crate. "Warm and cozy! We can all stay and live here happily ever after," she said.

Daisy looked around at the beautiful shimmering walls of Emmy's cottage. It was a very nice place to visit, but she was truly glad she didn't have to stay.

"Lord Feldspar and Lady Flamina say we have to leave on Monday," Jesse reminded Emmy.

"Oh, piffle!" Emmy said with a wave of her bright-green talons. "They will let you stay longer. His Lordship and Her Ladyship are crazy about me. There is even talk of their making me a member of the Aura."

"What's the Aura?" Daisy asked.

"The court of the Grand Beacons. Don't worry," Emmy chirped. "They'll warm to you, too. I wouldn't be surprised if they wound up letting you stay here forever."

"Forever is a long, long time, Em," said Daisy. "We'll talk about it more tomorrow. Right now, it's time for bed."

They tucked Emmy into her lava-sock-filled crate.

"Are there any books here for us to read to you?" Jesse asked. Even though Emmy was a lightning-fast reader, she still liked to be read to at bedtime.

Emmy shook her head. "The books in the Fiery Realm are like the computer, just pretend. I'll show you what we do here instead of reading books . . . tomorrow, because right now I'm sooooo sleepy. This has been such an exciting day."

Jesse and Daisy went next door to their own room. Daisy noticed that there was no bathroom, which was odd. Then again, she didn't have to go. Nor did she feel the need to wash her face or even brush her teeth. It was as if all activities involving water were out of the question, as if water itself had evaporated from existence here.

They climbed into their beds, and the room darkened to a deep maroon hue that reminded Daisy of the color of the insides of your eyelids as you're drifting off to sleep.

Jesse's voice sounded very close in the darkness. "It's like sleeping inside one of those blanket forts we used to make, isn't it, Daisy? Warm and cozy."

"It is," said Daisy.

Jesse yawned. "Do you think Emmy made a crate of socks for herself because she misses the one in the garage?"

"It's the only bed she's ever known." It was Daisy's turn to yawn. "This bed is so much more comfortable than mine," she said.

Jesse's voice came back at her, sharp with worry. "You're not thinking of sticking around any longer than we have to, are you?" he asked.

"Of course not!" Daisy said.

"Listen, Daze. I've lived in some pretty neat places, but you always wind up with scorpions in your shoes and snakes in your toilets, trust me. I *want* to live in Goldmine City. I did not sign on for this."

"Sign on?" Daisy said.

"You know what I mean," Jesse said. "Living in the gloaming like this. It's like being stuck inside a lava lamp. Besides, how great a world can it be if someone's going around swiping all those cute little fire fairies? Now let's get some sleep. I have a feeling we're going to need it."

The next morning, Jesse woke up with a pounding headache. He staggered out of bed and found the backpack sitting on top of the pretend computer. He pulled out the purple canteen and took a swig of Fiery Elixir. While it didn't taste quite as strong as it had before, he felt almost instantly better.

Daisy stirred in her bed. She rolled over and

groaned. Her face was hot pink against her pale-blond hair, her eyes bloodshot. "Feel my head. I think I might have a fever," she croaked.

"Here," Jesse said, holding out the canteen to her. "Have some of this. You'll feel better."

Daisy groped for the canteen and took a sip. She sat up and smacked her lips. "You're right!" she said, looking much more like herself again. "I feel fit as a fiddle."

"Fit as a *griddle,* you mean," Jesse said with a laugh.

Emmy appeared in their doorway. "How is everyone this morning?"

Daisy, about to repeat Jesse's joke, decided not to and said, "We're fine."

"Finer than fine," Jesse said. He could not remember ever having slept so well.

"You were going to show us what you do here instead of reading books," Daisy said.

"Oh, yes," Emmy said. "We do this." She waved her arm across the wall where the window overlooking the driveway would have been if they were at home. Suddenly, it was as if they were peering through the wall into the next room, where Aunt Maggie and Uncle Joe were pacing across a black-and-white-tiled kitchen, each jiggling a tiny, blanketed bundle. One of the babies was crying, and

Uncle Joe was singing a sweet, silly song to it. Somewhere nearby a teakettle rattled and whistled.

"I know where that is! That's my brother's kitchen on Mass. Avenue in Cambridge!" Daisy exclaimed.

"They don't seem to hear us," Jesse said. "How come we can see them?"

"Because they are standing in front of the gas stove, where there is a fire in the burner," Emmy said. She waved again. This time, they saw strangers in sombreros, bathed in the red glow of a campfire and singing a song in Spanish to the strains of a guitar. Another wave revealed fire trucks and a family lined up along a sidewalk, clutching pillowcases full of belongings, the reflection of their burning house shining in their wide, anxious eyes. More waves showed people blowing out birthday candles, lighting pipes, and mending fenders with welding torches. Jesse found it more than a little disturbing but also kind of mesmerizing, like staring into a fire.

"Wherever there is a fire in the Earthly Realm, we can see through to it," Emmy said. "It's called the Fire Screen. Everybody has one. The fire fairies love to watch the Fire Screen. They get almost all their decorating ideas from it."

"So how do you control what picture you're

going to see?" Jesse asked. "Is there some sort of remote channel changer?"

Emmy chuckled. "I use dragon magic," she said, waving and banishing the screen. "You probably won't have very much control. You might see something or someone familiar . . . or you might not."

"I wonder if that's what the professor was doing," Jesse said thoughtfully.

"When?" Daisy asked.

"Last time we saw him. When he was messing around with that pipe. Maybe he was looking in on Emmy in the Fiery Realm."

"Makes sense to me," Daisy said.

"Now come along, Keepers," Emmy said. "We're due at the royal runching. The fiery mote of my heart awaits me."

When they stepped out the door, Jesse said, "Nice night."

It was, in fact, every bit as dark as it had been when they went to bed.

"Do what I do," Daisy said. "Just pretend you're wearing sunglasses with dark-red lenses."

Jesse nodded and looked around with new eyes. "Okay," he said slowly, "that ought to work."

When they arrived at the Great Hall, they found that the throne room had been transformed into the world's biggest cafeteria. Acres of huge tables stretched out before them. The room roared and flamed with the sound of dragons and fire fairies all talking and laughing at once. One long table stood on a raised platform. Lady Flamina sat at one end and Lord Feldspar at the other, with an assortment of fire fairies and dragons seated in between.

"So this is a runching, eh?" Jesse said, looking around.

"A *royal* runching," Emmy said. "Jasper and I will be sitting up there with the Grand Beacons and their Aura, but my boons Opal and Galena will keep you company."

Emmy sat them at a table with her boons, and the three fire fairies, Spark, Flicker, and Fiero, soon flitted over to join them.

"Do you guys go everywhere together?" Jesse asked.

"We didn't use to," said Flicker. "But Lady Flamina says we younger fire fairies must now travel in groups . . . for safety's sake."

If there is safety in numbers, Jesse thought, looking around at the mob, *this is probably the safest place in the Fiery Realm right now*. He wound up seated between Opal and Fiero. Opal was talking to Daisy, so Jesse struck up a conversation with Fiero.

"So do all the fire fairies watch the Fire Screen?"

"Not only watch," said Fiero. "Some of us even lick in."

There was that word again. "What's 'lick in' mean?" Jesse asked.

"It means we can join up with the flame in the Earthly Realm and get ourselves a really good look at what's happening on your side of things," Fiero said.

"What she isn't telling you," Flicker put in shyly from across the table, "is that licking is considered very rude, because it causes reception problems on everyone else's Fire Screen."

"Oh, right," said Jesse, nodding. It was sort of like standing up in a theater and blocking the view of the person behind you.

The roar of the runchers rose to an even higher pitch. Two doors burst open, and a procession of fire fairies and dragons filed in bearing trays and platters piled high with food. Jesse, expecting the food to be weird, was pleasantly surprised to see all sorts of familiar-looking dishes: roast suckling pig and spaghetti with meatballs, hamburgers and hot dogs, tacos and Chinese dumplings, and even pizza pie. It might not be traditional breakfast food, but it looked delicious. A blue dragon draped in a voluminous white apron placed a platter of steaming roast turkey on their table. Bowls heaped with mashed potatoes, green peas, and yams followed.

"It's a Thanksgiving feast!" Jesse said, helping himself. "This tastes *great!*" he said after sampling a little of everything.

Daisy nodded enthusiastically and said, "Amazingly good!"

"The secret ingredient—in fact, the *only* ingredient," Galena said mildly, "is air."

Jesse and Daisy stopped with their forks halfway to their mouths. "Air?" they asked the lilac-hued dragon.

Galena nodded. "We're fire beings here, dragons and fairies alike," she explained. "All we need is oxygen to keep ourselves going. We whip the oxygen into other forms . . . just to make it more interesting . . . and runchable. We get most of our ideas from your world by watching the Fire Screen."

"Of course!" Jesse said. "Because we cook with fire, so you would see into kitchens all over the world. I bet it's sort of like watching the Food Channel."

Jesse dug in again but stopped when he saw that neither Galena nor Opal had touched her plate of food.

Daisy noticed, too. "Aren't you hungry?" she

asked, with the half-gnawed turkey drumstick halfway to her mouth.

"Actually," said Opal, the skin above her eyes rumpled with concern, "we wanted to talk to you about Emerald."

"What she means is," Galena said, "we're worried about what will happen when Jasper's fiery mote comes back from her patrol of the Outer Reaches."

"Whoa!" Daisy set down her turkey leg slowly. "You're telling us that Jasper already *has* a mote?"

CHAPTER SIX

LOOGIES OF FIRE

"So does Emmy know yet that Jasper has a girlfriend—um, mote?" Jesse asked.

Opal shook her head. "I don't think Jasper has the heart to tell her. He's afraid . . . of hurting her feelings."

"But won't it hurt her feelings worse the longer he waits?" Daisy said with a pained look on her face.

Jesse looked up at the dais. Emmy and Jasper, foreheads touching, were in a world of their own. It looked like nothing in this realm or any other could ever come between them.

"Emmy thinks they're TLFEE," Jesse said.

"What is that?" Galena said.

"True lovers for ever and ever," Daisy said with a contemptuous wave of her hand. "That's just some tripe he and Emmy read in *Shimmer*."

"What's tripe?" Opal asked.

"What's shimmer?" Galena wanted to know.

"Tripe is meaningless drivel, and *Shimmer* is a magazine that prints it," Jesse said.

"For Young Women in the Glow," Daisy added with a curl of her lip.

"Well, Emerald is certainly glowing," Opal said with a worried shake of her head.

"And it's all that rascal Jasper's doing," said Galena.

"The big two-timing galoot!" Daisy said, brandishing her drumstick.

"Shhhh," Jesse hissed. "Emmy and the big two-timing galoot are headed this way."

Emmy, strolling beside Jasper, approached their

table and said, "Are you cousins finished with your runching? Because Jasper and I are going to take you for a jaunt in the country."

Jesse and Daisy nodded dully. Suddenly, both of them had lost their appetites.

"The country is very different from the city," Emmy explained as, immediately following the runching, they made their way through the streets of the Ruby City toward the outskirts. Here the buildings were lower, though no less dazzling. "It is very wild and sometimes dangerous. You must stay close to me at all times."

Daisy said, "We'll be riding on your back, won't we?"

Daisy was already burning with jealousy of the fire fairies. The cheery little trio had ridden Emmy's tail all the way to where they now stood at the entrance to a sprawling structure made from ruby and clear quartz bricks. Its long, wide central aisle had stalls on either side. It looked like the stable of an important and very large king. Daisy couldn't see inside the stalls, but she could hear snorting and stomping, and the air was filled with glittery dust and smoke.

Emmy was shaking her head sadly. "Fire fairies hitchhiking on my tail is one thing, but *you* cannot ride me here in this place. The other dragons would

frown on it. It would be disrespectful to me. Dragons here are very proud. I must learn to have more
pride in myself if I am to stay."

"But we're your *Keepers*," Daisy protested.
"Can't they make an exception?"

"No exceptions allowed, but I have the perfect
mounts already chosen for you. Fire salamanders!"
Her green eyes shone with excitement as she flung
open two of the stall doors.

Two six-legged, alligator-size salamanders with
red and white stripes slewed out into the aisle.
Jesse let out a yip and jumped to one side.

"Meet Speedy and Clipper," Emmy said
proudly. "Aren't they sweet?"

Daisy gulped. In spite of their playful names
and their candy-cane stripes, the fire salamanders
were anything but sweet. Red ruffs wreathed their
massive heads, through the top of which smoke
puffed out of two holes. But Daisy didn't want to
spoil Emmy's surprise, so she said with grim deter-
mination, "What do we hold on to?"

"The ruffles," Emmy said. She reached down
and plucked playfully at the ruff surrounding Clipper's smoking head. Daisy was surprised to see that
Jesse was already gamely perched on Speedy's back,
leaning forward like a jockey braced for the starting
gun, baggy flaps of skin gathered up in each hand.

"Do these things fly?" Jesse asked, looking a little pale.

"No," said Emmy, "but they go like the wind, so hang on tight."

Daisy scrambled up on Clipper's back, which was smooth as snakeskin, warm, and a little slippery. Her feet dangled about a foot off the ground. She could feel the creature's ribs heaving beneath her and hear the rumbling of its guts. *This must be what it feels like to be on a revving motorcycle,* she thought. "Okay. So how do we get them to start and stop?" Daisy asked.

"Don't worry. They're herd animals. They'll go when Jasper and I go and stop when we stop," Emmy said.

Then they were off, the two fire salamanders neck and neck on the heels of the two bounding dragons.

Daisy was expecting a bumpy ride, so her hands clenched the ruff. She fixed her eyes on the fire fairies bouncing up and down on Emmy's tail, giving the impression even from a short distance that Emmy's tail had caught fire. But the ride turned out to be as smooth as velvet, and after a while Daisy's grip eased and she sat back and took in the sights as well as she could in the perpetually dim light.

Beneath the deep-maroon sky, pendulous blossoms and leaves as long as surfboards grew together in a vast, rubbery, steaming tangle, none of it green. Every so often, the jungle would thin out and reveal a cliff face of dazzling ruby or topaz or a towering butte of sparkling sapphire. Now and then, what Daisy took for a blossom would open its mouth and spit fire and shuffle off into the undergrowth. There were airborne insects here, too, igniting mid-flight like flicked matches, and birds swooping overhead on wings of flame.

It was a good thing the fire salamanders had a smooth gait, because Emmy and Jasper took turns chasing each other, bobbing and weaving and leading the fire salamanders on a merry, never-ending series of loop-de-loops. The jungle echoed with the sound of Jasper's jolly growl and Emmy's laughter, carefree and happy. Daisy would have given anything to share Emmy's joy, but all she could think was *What will happen when Jasper's fiery mote comes back?*

Jesse brought Speedy closer to Clipper. "If she and the big galoot are splitsville," he called out to Daisy, "it will be easier to get her to come home."

"How can you say that?" Daisy said. "Her heart will be broken! You remember what it's like when she cries."

Jesse nodded glumly. "There isn't a hand-kerchief huge enough to dry that many tears," he said.

Just then, Emmy circled back to them and cut short their talk. "Are you guys having fun yet?" she asked.

Jesse and Daisy plastered bright smiles across their faces and nodded like bobble-headed dolls.

"Great!" Jesse said.

"The time of our lives!" Daisy said.

Usually, Emmy could tell, even from the sound of their voices, when they were faking, but she was in such a hurry to get back to Jasper's side that she didn't even notice.

"We're losing her," Jesse said miserably. "Can't you feel it?"

"Please don't say that! It sounds like you're giving up," Daisy said. But the truth was, she felt it, too, and she could barely stand it. They were losing their dragon!

"We're almost there! Hang on!" Emmy called back to them.

They swooped into a deep valley, through which a gleaming purple stream meandered like a sparkling chain of amethyst. Down and down they rushed until they stopped on the banks of the stream. The fire fairies tumbled off Emmy's tail. Following suit, Jesse and Daisy dismounted from their fire salamanders, who scuttled off to graze on the fuzzy purple plants growing everywhere. Nearby, the stream boiled over amethyst boulders and cascaded into a bubbling lavender-colored basin.

"Watch this!" Emmy said. She ran up the embankment, dived into the rapids, bumped along on her tail, and spilled helter-skelter over the cliff into the pool. "Try it!" she said when her head bobbed up.

The fire fairies were already tumbling down the falls after Emmy, shouting and flaming and screaming with delight.

"Come on!" Jesse said to Daisy. "It looks like fun."

Daisy shook her head. "The big galoo—er, Jasper and I will sit here on the bank and have a little chitchat, won't we?"

Jasper rumbled in agreement. Jesse scrambled up the bank to the top of the falls and leaped into the boiling stream. Daisy watched as he disappeared over the edge. She breathed a sigh of relief when his head popped up in the pool. This time, the smile on his face was genuine.

"That was great!" he said breathlessly. "Better

than any amusement park ride I've ever been on. Who knew shooting lava rapids could be such a blast?"

"Clear the way!" Emmy called out from above. "I don't want to land on you and squish you flat, Jesse Tiger. Bombs away!"

Jesse kicked clear just as Emmy rode the falls over the brink and tumbled, head over heels, into the pool. Then Jesse and Emmy and the fire fairies took turn after turn, riding the fire falls with tireless enthusiasm. Daisy sat and watched them, waiting for the right words to start a conversation with Jasper.

At length, Jasper said, "Emmy's a brilliant boon."

"She seems very fond of you," Daisy said carefully.

Emmy was waving to Jasper from the top of the lava falls.

"Come out and runch!" Jasper called up to her.

"Just one more ride!" she called back.

Jasper sighed, as if greatly put upon. "I fear she is far too taken with me," he said. "But it will pass."

"How can you be so sure?" Daisy said.

Jasper avoided meeting Daisy's eyes.

"Look at her," Jasper said, "playing with the young ones. In some ways she's worldly, but in other ways, she is still a small child. She's not ready for the rigors of motehood."

Daisy saw her opportunity. "But your real fiery mote is?"

Jasper nodded and sighed as if that relationship offered very little joy.

"When were you planning to tell Emmy about you and . . . her?"

"She'll find out about Malachite soon enough," he said. "She-dragons compete constantly for my favors. The trouncings are frequent and furious, I'm afraid."

So the big galoot is stuck-up, too! Daisy thought, anger prickling her scalp.

"It's not what you think," said Jasper, reading her expression. "It's just that there are four she-dragons for every he-dragon in the realm. I am used to them trouncing each other to win my favors."

"I see," said Daisy, not sure how to feel. She wondered if Emmy would see and whether it would make losing Jasper any easier when the time came. Daisy doubted it. And what if Emmy got trounced? It didn't sound like being trounced was any fun at all. It might even be dangerous.

After everyone had ridden the lava falls until they were dizzy and spent, they sprawled on the bank and had a picnic runch.

Daisy noticed Emmy wasn't runching. "Aren't you hungry?" she asked.

"I'll just make do with pure air," Emmy said merrily. She was busy collecting the amethyst pebbles that lined the streambed.

"What are you making?" Jesse asked. He had inhaled his oxygen BLT. Riding the lava stream had made him ravenous.

"A little something . . . for the dance tonight!" she said with a wink at Jasper.

"We had better start back," Jasper said, "if we don't want to be late for the Fire Ball."

The dragons helped Jesse and Daisy back onto their fire salamanders, the fairies flitted onto Emmy's tail, and together they set off for the Ruby City. Overhead, the sky had deepened to the color of ripe eggplant. The jungle writhed and twisted around them, darker and more sinister than it had seemed earlier. Jesse heard menacing hissing and thumping in the undergrowth, followed by an ear-piercing shriek. Speedy wallowed and whipped his head around. Two giant beasts reared up behind them. They looked like lions, only five times bigger and raging red, ringed with manes of fire.

The lions put up their backs and spat at Speedy. Speedy screamed and lashed his tail as the fire lions pounced. Emmy smacked Speedy's haunch to get him going, but Speedy had frozen with fear. Then Jesse saw why. The lions had flamed him. His long red and white tail was now a smoldering stump.

"These things spit fire!" Daisy said, her eyes wide.

"Loogies of fire!" Jesse said ominously.

"Jesse Tiger, kick Speedy and make him giddyup and get away from the fire loogies!" Emmy cried.

Jesse booted Speedy's flanks with all his might and felt the beast come to life beneath him, felt the heat of the lions' fiery breath lessen. Jesse looked back and saw Jasper drawing the lions away from the salamanders. He roared and a gout of flame shot out of his mouth.

Jesse stared, slack-jawed. He knew that some dragons breathed fire, but actually witnessing the phenomenon was something else altogether. Dragon and lions exchanged rounds, Jasper a fierce flamethrower to their meager little flares. Eventually, Jasper's flame drove the fire lions back into the jungle.

"Speedy lost his tail!" Jesse said when they were safely away from the fire lions and back on their way again.

Emmy said, "Don't fret. Speedy's tail will grow back."

"I don't get it," Jesse said. "This is the Fiery Realm. Everything's on fire. How can flame hurt anyone here?"

"It isn't the flame. It's the acid in the flame," Emmy said. "It burns hotter than fire and disintegrates flesh."

"Except for salamanders' tails," Daisy said.

"Fire salamanders' tails are the exception," Emmy said. "That's why they make such trusty mounts."

"All the same," said Daisy, "I prefer Old Bub."

Back at the cottage, Emmy and Daisy went to Emmy's room to get ready for the Fire Ball. Alone in the bedroom, Jesse went over to the wall where Emmy had shown them the pictures on the Fire Screen. He waved his arm.

Miss Alodie instantly appeared, holding a teacup, hunkered down on Uncle Joe's easy chair in the living room before the fireplace. In a high, sweet voice, she was singing, *"Fire's burning! Fire's burning! Draw nearer! Draw nearer!"*

Jesse joined in: *"In the gloaming! In the gloaming! Come sing and be merry!"*

As he sang and watched the screen, Jesse felt a pang of homesickness. Behind Miss Alodie, the shelves rose up, weighted down with the familiar jumble of books and Uncle Joe's rocks. Jesse saw the reflection of the fire sparkling in Miss Alodie's blue eyes. *It would be nice to be there with her,* he thought, *safe and sound.*

"There you are!" said Miss Alodie when the song was over. "I've been waiting for one of you to show up all afternoon."

Startled, Jesse pointed to himself. "You can see me!" he said.

"Of course I can! I'm an old Pyromantic from way back. You can see all kinds of things in a fire if you settle down and take the time to look," Miss Alodie said, "which most folks don't."

"I think we're going to be staying here at least until Monday," Jesse said.

"Like I said, stay as long as you need to, but I thought you should see this," she said. She put down her teacup and held up something round and flat. Jesse squinted and leaned closer to the Fire Screen to see what it was. It was the Toilet Glass, from their Museum of Magic collection! The lid was open and the ancient silvery mirror flashed in the firelight.

"I went up to the barn when you didn't come home," Miss Alodie said. "And I found this thing lying on the floor—open."

"Well, shut it!" Jesse said. "We're holding the

Princess Sadra captive in that thing."

"Not anymore we aren't, kiddo," said Miss Alodie, closing the compact with a loud snap. "She's escaped."

Jesse felt panic bubbling up in him. "Are you sure?"

"As sure as sure can be," Miss Alodie said grimly. She leaned forward in her chair, her face deep scarlet as she neared the fire. "You Keepers be careful now, do you hear me? I'll tell you what I think is going on—"

Just then, a shadow fell across the Fire Screen and blotted out the picture as well as the sound. Jesse knew what was happening. Someone from the Fiery Realm was licking in and interfering with reception. Jesse waited a few moments for whomever it was to clear off. But when they didn't, he couldn't help thinking that whoever was doing the licking was doing so on purpose, either to eavesdrop or to keep Miss Alodie from telling Jesse what he and Daisy needed to know. He waved his arm and made the Fire Screen disappear. Then he went next door to tell Daisy.

Daisy was doing elegant pirouettes across the floor. A beautiful gown swirled around her with skirts like moonlight on sea foam. Her hair was caught up in a glittering clip. She looked like Clara in *The Nutcracker.*

Daisy leaped gracefully in the air and landed lightly before him. "Do you like my dress, Jess? It's got fire opals woven into the hem. And look at my slippers!"

She pointed a toe. The slippers were pearly satin, with tiny topazes, emeralds, and moonstones forming a design of daisies. She performed another pirouette, then curtseyed deeply. Jesse couldn't believe his eyes. Daisy had always wanted to dance, just like she wanted to figure skate, but as she herself often said, she had all the grace of a frog jumping off a flat rock. What had happened to her?

CHAPTER SEVEN

THE FIRE BALL

"I made the dress and slippers myself," Daisy said.

Jesse was bewildered. "Since when can you sew?"

"Since now. In this place, I can make anything I want . . . with my own hands. I can whomp up a

gown and slippers. Oh, Jess! These slippers make
me feel so light on my feet. I feel like I could dance
the lead in *Swan Lake*! But I'll settle for going to the
Fire Ball."

"Isn't your Daisy-cousin beautiful?" Emmy
asked. Emmy herself was all dolled up, in an elabo-
rate headdress and veil made from the amethysts
she had found in the stream.

"You both look great," Jesse said. He was so be-
dazzled, in fact, that he nearly forgot why he had
come in here in the first place. "But we need to
talk."

"*You* need to get ready for the ball." Daisy
folded her arms and stared critically at his blue
jeans and T-shirt. "You weren't planning on wearing
that, were you?"

Jesse looked down at himself. "Sure, why not?"

"Because it's not *finery*," Emmy put in. "There's
a dress code. Opal and Galena say finery is called
for."

Jesse groaned.

"Don't worry. I'll whomp something up for you!"
Daisy said brightly. "All of that neat stuff we saw in
the shop windows in the Ruby City? It was just
for show. People don't shop in stores here. When
they want something, they just pull it out of thin air.
Like this!"

Jesse watched as Daisy weaved her fingers around him. He looked down at himself. Suddenly, he was wearing a shiny golden jacket with epaulets made of silvery fringe.

"Wow!" He didn't know what else to say. He looked like a Las Vegas performer.

Daisy stood back and squinted. "Needs a little something else." She weaved her hands some more and sparkly white trousers with a knife-edge crease replaced his jeans. A sweep of her hands across his chest left tiers of jeweled medals in its wake. Now he looked *really* ridiculous. But Daisy seemed so pleased with her handiwork, he didn't want to spoil her mood.

"Thanks, Daisy. I look . . . *resplendent*," he said.

"You look better than that, Jesse Tiger!" Emmy said with a grin. "You look *hot*."

"Um, news bulletin, Em? *Everybody* is hot here in the Fiery Realm," Jesse said, Then to Daisy, he added: "*Now* can we talk?"

"No time now to talk!" Emmy said, clapping her talons together briskly. "We'll be late for the Fire Ball. Come along, you two wow-wows. It's red carpet time in the Ruby City!"

"Isn't Jasper coming to pick you up?" Jesse asked.

"Jasper said he would meet me at the dance," Emmy said.

Jesse frowned deeply. Weren't dates supposed to pick you up at your house? Jesse would have to have a little talk with Jasper.

Jesse trailed behind Emmy and Daisy along the diamond-paved path that led beneath the city gates. Daisy kept running ahead and leaping, clicking her heels, spinning in midair, and landing with her arms raised as gracefully as a prima ballerina.

"Admit it, Jesse Tiger. I'm amazing!" Daisy said, happy and breathless.

"You're amazing," Jesse said. "But we still need to talk."

"Later!" Daisy said, bounding off. "Don't you want to dance?"

"No, thanks," said Jesse. As much as Daisy wanted to dance, Jesse did not. Perhaps it was because he wasn't wearing dancing clothes. He peered beneath the white trouser cuffs and saw that he still wore sneakers. For a minute, he thought about whomping himself up some dancing slippers so that he could keep Daisy company, but then he thought again. *I don't want to dance. I want to talk to Daisy about what I saw and heard on the Fire Screen.*

The streets of the Ruby City were teeming with dragons all converging on the same spot. Now that Jesse knew the ratio of male to female dragons, it seemed like every dragon he saw was female. Like Emmy, all had draped jeweled veils over their horns. They looked like hefty maidens from the Middle Ages. The males strutted along with medallions on ribbons around their necks, looking like ambassadors on their way to a diplomatic banquet.

Golden light blazed out of a building that looked like a towering ruby-bricked silo. The front doors, carved in the shape of two golden harps, stood wide open. Jesse and Daisy and Emmy entered and looked around. Daisy wondered how all the dragons were going to fit in the small amount of floor space, much less dance together. Rising to a dizzying height were tier upon tier of balconies draped with garlands of sparkling crystals. Mysteriously, there were no doors or stairs or ramps leading to the many balconies. Were they just for decoration? Then she saw that one balcony held a quintet of fire fairies playing crystal instruments that produced a sprightly melodic tune. It sounded like wind pinging a row of icicles.

"Come on! Let's dance," Daisy said, her feet already moving. Then she saw a dragon couple dancing, their feet hovering six feet off the ground, and her feet stopped in their tracks. Jesse saw, too. How odd to see dragons, so huge and heavy on the ground, floating gracefully and gravity-free.

"Emmy, I thought you said the dragons of the Fiery Realm couldn't fly," Jesse said.

"They can't. They're just floating," said Emmy, a crafty gleam in her eye. "Follow me."

Emmy led them over to a small fountain in the wall spouting bluish-green foam. Next to the fountain there was a stack of large crystal bowls. She held first one bowl, then another, beneath the outflow until they were filled to the brim with the blue-green foam.

"Have some bubbly!" Emmy said, holding out the bowls.

"We're way too young for champagne," said Jesse.

"It's not champagne," said Emmy. "That's what it's called. *Bubbly.* Try some."

Jesse and Daisy each gingerly cradled a sloshing bowl. Jesse brought it to his lips. The bubbles tickled his nose. He flicked his tongue in and instantly puckered up. The drink possessed the gland-prickling tartness of fresh limes.

"Interesting," said Daisy, nose wrinkled, taking another sip. Jesse watched as Daisy's feet rose up off the floor.

"Whoa!" said Jesse, his eyes following her. "Don't look now, Daze, but you're airborne."

"So are you!" said Daisy, pointing at him and giggling. They each took a couple more sips and rose several more inches off the floor, until they were level with the first balcony tier. So *that's* how you got to the balconies!

"Look at us!" said Daisy giddily. "Now I'll be *really* light-footed! Let's dance, Jess!"

They parked their bowls on the balcony rail and launched into the kind of dancing Jesse liked best, hooking elbows and swinging each other around and around. Unhampered by gravity, they threw in backflips and somersaults, laughing fit to burst.

The silo was now dense with dragons. Most of them were hovering in the air, stacked up clear to the ceiling. Jasper and Emmy were in the thick of it, spinning each other around like sparkling tops.

Breathless, Jesse finally managed to reel Daisy over to the side of the room, where they bumped up softly against the balcony like a couple of stray helium-filled balloons. "I saw Miss Alodie on the Fire Screen earlier," Jesse said breathlessly.

Daisy's eyes went wide. She grabbed him by his gold lamé lapel and hauled him in. "You did? Why didn't you tell me?"

"What do you think I've been trying to do, but you've been too busy having fun to listen," Jesse said.

"I'm listening now," Daisy said.

Jesse said, "Miss Alodie wanted to warn us that Sadra escaped from the Toilet Glass."

"Yikes! We've got to get home fast and find her," Daisy said, race-walking in midair, as if that might bring her back to the Earthly Realm or, at the very least, down to the floor. It did, in fact, do neither of these things.

"That's just it," Jesse said. "She was just about to tell me more when someone licked in and blocked her out. And, Daze, I had the feeling it wasn't an accident."

"You mean someone from here?" Daisy looked around, as if the ballroom had been transformed into a nest of spies. "Jeez! How are we supposed to get down from here? We can't do anything until we get our feet back on the ground."

Jesse spied Opal and Galena, who were standing over by the door. Skating through the air, he towed Daisy along behind him until they were directly over the heads of the boons. Opal's horns were dressed with pearls and Galena's with beads of pale pink. "Hey, pssssst, ladies!" Jesse called down to them.

Opal looked up. "Hello, Keepers! I see you've joined in the festivities!"

"Yeah, but can you help us get down?" Daisy asked.

Opal reached up and hauled Jesse and Daisy down to earth by their ankles. Then she kept them anchored with a paw on each head.

"Thanks, Opal. But it looks like you're going to have to hold us down for the rest of the evening," Daisy said.

"No, she won't," Galena said, and that's when she began to pound Jesse, then Daisy, hard on the back as if they were a couple of babies with the colic. Soon enough, first Jesse, then Daisy, let out with a rippingly large and very loud belch.

Opal removed her paws from the tops of their heads. All four of their feet remained flat on the floor.

"Neat trick!" said Daisy.

"Easier than I thought it would be!" Jesse said.

"I stay away from the bubbly myself," said Opal. "Me, I like to keep my feet firmly planted on the ground."

"Me too," said Galena. "Especially tonight."

Jesse was just about to ask Galena why especially tonight when the golden harp doors swung open.

A statuesque smoky-green dragon strode into the room and looked around. She had not just two but seven horns sprouting from the top of her head in a sort of spiky crown, like the Statue of Liberty, only a great deal less warm and welcoming-looking.

Four more dragons, with three horns apiece, followed the smoky-green dragon into the ballroom and lined up along the walls, two on either side of the doorway, staring at the gathering with cold eyes.

The music collapsed like a wall of breaking glass. The dragon dancers shrank away against the walls, stuffed themselves into the nearest balcony seats, and looked down in nervous anticipation, transforming the space almost instantly from ballroom to arena. Emmy and Jasper continued to spin each other around, even after the room had fallen into silence.

The smoky-green dragon with the crest of horns narrowed her eyes at the lone dancing couple. She walked over to the fountain and drank from it. The crowd gasped as the smoky-green dragon rose up several heads higher than the dancing couple and stared down at them in distaste.

"That's her, isn't it?" Daisy whispered to Opal, looking up with dread.

"That's Malachite, all right!" said Opal.

"Mean as a fire lion with her mane caught in an

air vent," said Galena. "And she's brought her rumble with her."

"What's a rumble?" Jesse whispered.

"Her boons. They go everywhere with her," Opal said.

"Those four tough dragons standing against the wall with the smoke curling out of their nostrils?" Daisy asked.

"The very ones," said Galena. "Oh, I wouldn't tangle with any of them. Trounce you as soon as look at you."

"Emerald of Leandra!" Malachite spoke in a loud, clear voice.

Jasper stopped midspin. "Malachite!" he said, looking up. He quickly put Emmy behind him as if attempting to shield her.

"Stand aside, Jasper," Malachite said. "My business is with Emerald, not with you, my foolish, philandering mote."

"Hello, Malachite!" Emmy said, gazing upward with touching eagerness. "It's so nice to meet you."

Malachite said coldly, "Are you ready to submit yourself to a trouncing to back your claim on the fiery mote of my heart?"

From their balcony seats, the dragons murmured amongst themselves.

"Of *your* heart?" Emmy said. "That's funny. I

thought he was the mote of *my* heart."

"I keep telling you," Jasper muttered from behind Emmy. "We're just boons."

"Boons don't dance together at the Fire Ball," Malachite said. Then, eyes flashing at Emmy, she said, "I challenge you, Emerald of Leandra, to a trouncing."

Emmy shrugged and said, "Then I guess I accept."

The dragons howled and hooted in approval, banging the tops of the chairs in front of them like unruly children at a movie matinee.

Jasper spoke up, his voice soft and pleading. "Malachite, I beg you to understand. Emmy doesn't know what she's saying. She is a stranger to our ways."

"I think not," said Malachite, sizing up Emmy. "She may be small and an insipid shade of green, but she is nobody's fool."

She flexed her forepaws and eight black talons shot out, as sharp and lethal-looking as the barbs on a set of medieval battle clubs. Then Emmy shot out her talons, sharp and green as rose thorns. Talons splayed, the two began to circle each other.

Up in the balconies, the dragons buzzed, speculating as to who the winner would be. Surely Malachite, with her size and experience and her dozens of victorious trouncings, had the edge. They continued to circle, Emmy looking up at Malachite, her green eyes alert and wary.

"Malachite's higher. This isn't a fair fight!" Jesse whispered furiously to Daisy.

"I know, but what can we do about it?" she whispered back.

Jesse ran over to the waterfall of bubbly and filled a bowl full. He drank enough of it to bring himself up level with Emmy, then quickly air-skated over and delivered the rest of the cup to her. "Quick, Em!" he said. "Drink it down!"

Without taking her eyes off Malachite, Emmy emptied the cup and handed it back to Jesse as she rose up level with the smoky-green dragon.

Jesse swallowed air and coaxed out a burp. He fell a few inches. Another burp came and he fell a few more inches. Before long, he was back on the floor next to Daisy, who patted his shoulder and said, "That was good thinking, Jess."

"Oh, I am afraid she's going to need more than bubbly to withstand a trouncing from Malachite," Opal said with a worried rattle of her headdress.

Just then, Malachite snarled and hurled herself at Emmy. There was a loud crackle of scales colliding, followed by a blur of limbs and tails, flashing dull and emerald green. Finally, they drew apart, their breath rasping in their chests, eyes fiercely locked.

Daisy cried out. Emmy had three long scratches down her front. She was bleeding!

"Don't worry," Galena whispered to Daisy, but she didn't sound very convincing.

Opal leaned in. "You should know that Malachite has never failed to triumph in a trouncing," she offered.

"Does this kind of thing happen here all the time?" Jesse asked.

"Trouncing is the way she-dragons prove their worthiness to their motes," Opal explained. "Malachite knows she must fight to hold on to her mote. She is happy to defend what is hers."

"What a world!" Daisy muttered darkly.

The dragons closed in on each other and tangled once again, tails thrashing. When they separated, Emmy grabbed hold of Malachite's tail and swung her around. She let go and sent Malachite flying, smashing headlong into the nearest balcony. Malachite sagged against the rail, panting.

Daisy, Jesse, Opal, and Galena cheered, while everyone else was still and silent, watching and waiting. A dragon in the balcony leaned forward and poked at Malachite, urging her to return to the fray.

Malachite shook her great horned head, drew herself up, and flew at Emmy, scratching and punching and kicking and pummeling, driving Emmy down and down until Emmy's tail rested on the floor.

Malachite drew back. Slowly, Emmy began to rise up the wall. But it was the bubbly moving her, not her own power. Emmy looked beaten and completely done in. One beautiful emerald eye was nearly swollen shut.

Daisy dug her nails into Jesse's arm.

Malachite, seeing that Emmy was in a weakened state, came at her, talons bristling. At the last moment, Emmy braced herself against the wall, and repelled Malachite with a mighty thrust of her hind legs, sending the dragon crashing into a crystal swag, which exploded and rained down like sleet.

Malachite bounced off the floor, snorted, and shook the crystals from her scales. Smoke shot out of her nostrils in two long gray streams.

"Uh-oh! Emmy's done it now," Opal said. "She's made Malachite mad."

"Look out, Emmy!" Jesse shouted.

Puffing like a locomotive, Malachite came on, chugging and growling. Emmy edged toward the doorway.

Opening her mouth wide, Malachite shot out

a column of flame like the mighty jet from an acetylene torch and drove Emmy, limbs flailing, from the building.

The room was silent, engulfed in smoke. A scorched trail ran across the floor and disappeared out the door. The air smelled charred. Black smoke curled from Malachite's nostrils and lips and ears. She shook her horned head and let out a mighty roar of triumph that rattled the crystal swags. The balconies erupted in thunderous cheers.

Jesse and Opal and Galena fled outside. Daisy remained behind to see what happened next.

The cheering died away quickly. Malachite, her breath whistling in her chest, looked around as if daring the next challenger. Over in the corner, Jasper shook his head bleakly and sighed.

Daisy spoke up. "Trouncing is a nasty custom," she said. Then, facing off with the smoky-green dragon, she added, "And if Jasper chooses you above Emmy, as far as I'm concerned, you two deserve each other!"

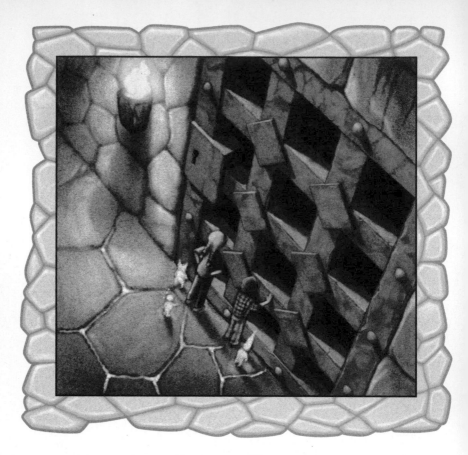

CHAPTER EIGHT

THE RUSTY HOOSEGOW

Emmy lay on the street whimpering, her scales seared black where Malachite had blasted her.

Jesse and Daisy didn't know what to do. It wasn't the wounds to her flesh that worried them so much as the damage to her spirit. Not since she was a tiny dragon coiled up in the sock drawer had they seen her in such a state of despair. Their party clothes had vanished, replaced by their jeans and T-shirts, which seemed appropriate. The Fire Ball was over. There would be no more dancing or bubbly tonight.

"We never should have let her stay here," Jesse said as they followed Opal and Galena, who bore Emmy's body between them, back to the cottage.

"It's not that simple," Daisy said. "She's older now, Jess. We can't just boss her around. She has a mind of her own."

"Yeah, and look where it got her!" Jesse said. "We should have done a better job of protecting her from herself. Isn't that what our parents do for us?"

"Only if we let them," Daisy said with a grim smile.

When they got back to the cottage, they tucked Emmy into her crate. At first, she was too shocked to do anything but lie there. But after a while, she began to weep. She tossed about, flinging lava socks everywhere. Tears dripped from her eyes, rolled down her nose, and fell on her chest wounds with a sound like cold rain hitting a hot sidewalk. Daisy ran to the backpack to get a bandanna and the small first aid kit they kept in the side pouch.

"There's no need to blot the tears," Galena said softly when she saw what Daisy was up to. "Dragon tears heal wounds."

"Oh!" said Daisy, staring at Jesse.

Jesse's eyes were round with wonder. It was good to know that Emmy had the power to heal herself, since there probably wasn't enough first aid cream in the whole tube to cover even one of the angry red scratches striping her chest and her shoulders, not to mention the burns.

"If she cries enough—and who could blame her?—she'll be fine by the morning. The tears will work their healing magic. It's her heart that will be slower to mend," said Opal.

Opal and Galena, seeing Emmy settled in, took their leave.

"We're going to look in on Jasper," they said. "Poor fellow."

"Jasper!" Daisy said, flaring up. "That two-timing galoot doesn't deserve your sympathy."

"*Everyone* deserves sympathy," Opal said, "even Jasper."

"Do you think it's easy being the mote of Malachite?" Galena said.

The very mention of Malachite sent Emmy into renewed fits of grief and shame.

"Please don't feel bad," Daisy said gently, stroking Emmy.

"You're a *beautiful* green," Jesse said. "Not insipid at all."

"What's more," Daisy added, "there are plenty more dragons just as nice as Jasper."

"Well," said Jesse, remembering the four-to-one ratio, "one or two, probably, at least."

"There will never be anyone but Jasper for me!" Emmy wailed.

The cousins took turns watching over Emmy until she fell into a shuddering slumber. They dabbed the surplus tears on the shoulder wounds the tears had missed. Then they dragged themselves to their beds and fell into an exhausted sleep.

In the morning, Jesse woke up with Daisy shaking him.

"Where's the canteen?" she asked.

Jesse blinked and looked around. "It's in the backpack, where I left it yesterday morning," he said in a hoarse voice.

"No, it's not," said Daisy. She closed her eyes. "I'm trying to remember whether it was in the backpack when I went to get the bandanna and first aid kit."

"Well, it's not there now," Jesse said, after he

checked for himself. "Who could have taken it?"

"Someone who wanted us to die a horrible death," Daisy suggested.

"Maybe not. Maybe Emmy took it to keep it safe," Jesse said.

They both went next door to Emmy's room. The crate was empty and socks were scattered everywhere. They searched the cottage. There was no sign of Emmy or the canteen. They stumbled out onto the front porch and looked around in the everlasting dimness. Just then, Spark, Flicker, and Fiero came flitting up the path.

"Good day, Keepers! You missed all the excitement!" Fiero said, bouncing up and down like a red rubber ball.

"After you left the Fire Ball last night, Jasper and Malachite butted horns," Spark said.

"Jasper told Malachite she was no longer the fiery mote of his heart," Flicker said tremulously.

"You mean they're splitsville?" Jesse said.

Fiero said, "Afterward, we followed Jasper when he stormed off. He was headed here. But on the way, the Grand Beacons' guard caught him and marched him off to the hole."

"To the hole?" Jesse and Daisy echoed.

"The Grand Beacons have accused him of *high*

treason!" Spark said, his little yellow flame coming to a sharp point.

"They say he is the leader of a group out to overthrow the Beacons and the Aura," Flicker said.

"Personally," Fiero said, "I don't think the big galoot has it in him. Jasper's *nice,* a boon to the entire realm. Not a rebel."

"So we came here right away to tell Emmy the news," said Flicker. "You two were fast asleep, so we went with her to the hole. She spoke with Jasper and, after that, she stormed off."

"All in all, there's been a great deal of storming off going on," Fiero said.

"We tried to tag along, but she shook us off her tail and told us to beat it," Spark said.

"Oh, she was on fire with rage," Fiero said.

"Out for revenge, she was," said Spark.

"We have to find out where she went," Flicker said. "She might need our help."

"But meanwhile, we're going to have to stick with you two," Fiero said. "Without Emmy's protection, we might get fairy-napped!"

"Well, we're in no shape to help anyone," Daisy said. "Someone stole our canteen of Fiery Elixir."

"Oh, that!" said Fiero, going round and rosy as a

ripe apple. "You don't need that stuff now. You've been here long enough. You're runching on air and living in lava. You're one of us as long as you want to stay here. Lady Flamina just said that to get you going."

"Oh, believe me, we'd love to get going if we could," Daisy said. "But not without our dragon."

"Let's go see if we can pay Jasper a visit in the clink," said Jesse.

"The clink?" said Daisy.

"Yeah, you know, from the gangster movies," said Jesse. Uncle Joe watched a lot of old black-and-white gangster movies, and sometimes Jesse sat in. "The pokey. The prison. The slammer. The big house. The can. The hoosegow?"

"Follow us," said Fiero, chuckling, "and we'll show you the way to the rusty hoosegow."

The fire fairies seemed incapable of being anything but cheery regardless of the situation, which Daisy found a comfort. As they were making their way to the Great Hall, she noticed that she had no headache. Considering the disturbing news, she felt remarkably good. Tingling all over, in fact. She looked over at Jesse. He looked good, too. His hair was shining and his cheeks were glowing. She noticed that her skin felt hot, but in a good way. She lifted her arm and pulled up the sleeve.

"Holy moly! Look, Jesse!" Daisy held out her arm.

The nearly invisible, pale-blond hairs on her arm looked like miniature candles with tiny flames on the tips. Jesse pushed up his sleeve and held his arm out next to hers. His arm hairs looked much the same way.

"Whoa!" he said.

Daisy said, "We're on fire, Jesse!"

"Well, fire or no fire, we still have to get back home before the weekend's over," Jesse said.

Daisy nodded. Only their second day here and already Goldmine City seemed like a place from another life. They arrived at the Great Hall of the Grand Beacons, where they rattled the pink quartz gate until the towering fire fairy guard with the golden staff marched down the stairs.

"We need to pay Jasper a visit in the hoosegow," Jesse said.

The guard looked perplexed. "The hoosegow?" he asked.

"Yeah," said Daisy, leaning on the gate, "the pokey, the slammer, the big house, the can, the pen, the prison! See where I'm going with this, buster?"

"Ah, the *hole*, you mean!" said the guard. "Well, you can't, by order of the Grand Beacons." He swung around and marched back up the stairs.

Jesse hollered after him, "In that case, we want to see the Beacons!"

The guard hesitated, spun around, and came marching back. "Very well. The court is in session, and all are welcome to an audience with Their Beneficent Beaconships."

The cousins and the fire fairies trooped down the long hallway that reminded Daisy of the gullet of a long-necked monster. In the great chamber, they found Lady Flamina and Lord Feldspar enthroned, as before. With Jasper not there to speak on their behalf, Daisy decided to get right down to cases and skip the dithering details, as Lady Flamina herself might say.

"We understand Jasper is being held prisoner here," Daisy said.

"We'd like to speak with him," Jesse said.

Lady Flamina flared up bright orange. "Jasper is a traitor being held in the hole. He is allowed no visitors until his trial."

"Well, apparently you let our dragon, Emerald of Leandra, visit him late last night," Jesse said.

"Afterward, she stormed off someplace," Daisy added. "We're hoping Jasper can tell us where she went."

"We realize this might be beyond your feeble powers of perception," said Jesse, "but we just want our dragon."

"Your upstart dragon must have connived her way past the night guards," Lord Feldspar grumbled.

"Had we known the upstart was on the premises, we would have detained her," said Lady Flamina. "She has been named a co-conspirator in the plot to overthrow the Grand Beacons."

"That's just ridiculous!" said Jesse.

Daisy's blood boiled. "Who says our dragon's a traitor?"

"A most reliable source," Lady Flamina said, simmering back down to a cool, calm blue.

"Who?" Jesse pressed.

"Yeah," Daisy said. "Jasper—and Emmy—are entitled to know the name of their accuser. That's the law in *our* realm, at least."

"Their accuser is my daughter!" Lord Feldspar thundered.

"The one who patrols the Outer Reaches and keeps us secure," Lady Flamina said.

It dawned on Daisy who the accuser was. "If you're talking about Malachite, then I wouldn't believe a word she said."

"Malachite? Trustworthy?" Jesse piped up. "I wouldn't trust her to babysit my parakeet long enough for me to clean the cage."

The Grand Beacons conferred in low voices. When they pulled apart, Lady Flamina delivered their decision in her coolest, bluest tones: "Very well, the Grand Beaconship of the Fiery Realm has revised its thinking. We will grant you visitation rights, briefly."

"Thanks!" the cousins said together.

"I wonder why the Beaconship changed their minds so quickly," Daisy said as a guard escorted them from the throne room.

"If you want," Fiero whispered, "we can lick back and spy for you."

"Please don't do that," said Jesse. "There's no use you winding up in the hoosegow, too."

The guard stopped when they came to a large black hole in the floor. "The prisoner is down there," he said, pointing.

Jesse leaned over and peered into the shaft. A rusty spiral staircase wound its way down into pitch darkness.

"Go on down," the guard said. "Jasper is the only prisoner down there. You can't miss him."

"Do we get to take a torch or something with us?" Daisy asked.

The guard shook his head. "Visitors are responsible for providing their own illumination."

Jesse looked at Daisy. She had that queasy look she got before entering dark, enclosed spaces. He wasn't crazy about them himself, but he hated them a little less than she did. The fire fairies spilled down the stairway and disappeared into the blackness. Jesse squared his shoulders and stepped down into the hole. Soon after, he heard Daisy's feet on the rusty stairs above his head.

"You okay?" he called up to her.

"I'll be fine," she said bravely. "My arms are glowing. Are yours?"

Jesse looked at his wrist. He didn't wear a watch these days, except to school, but his arm was shining as if he were wearing a glow-in-the-dark wristband. He rolled up the cuffs of his jeans and his ankles glowed, lighting his way to the next step.

"I wonder how Emmy got down these stairs," Daisy said.

"Or any dragon," Jesse said. "They're small . . . and they're iron."

Down and down the spiral staircase wound, around and around, an endless corkscrew. At the bottom, it felt hot and airless and silent, like the engine room of a giant ship with its power switched off. Jesse stood aside and waited for Daisy to join him. The fire fairies flitted ahead down the hot, narrow stone corridor.

"They seem to know their way around the hole," Jesse commented.

They followed the fire fairies and made their way past a long, gloomy procession of empty cells. Finally, they came upon Jasper. He lay on a bed of ashes, next to a feeble lantern, behind a stout, rusty grate.

"Pssst, Jasper!" Jesse called out to him through the grate.

Jasper got up and lumbered over. His proud shoulders were slumped, and his great golden eyes were sad. Jesse noticed he stood well back from the iron grate that separated them.

Jasper spoke in a low voice. "I'm sorry, Keepers. When Malachite told me to make a mote of Emmy, I never realized—"

"Malachite *told* you to?" Daisy said.

"She *ordered* me," Jasper said. "She has won so many trouncings over time, I have allowed her to dominate me."

"Poor Emmy," Jesse said under his breath. "She was set up."

"I don't get it. If it was Malachite's idea, why did she challenge Emmy to a trouncing?" Daisy said.

Jasper shrugged. "To weaken her, perhaps. Or just for fun."

"Some fun," Daisy said glumly.

"After the fight, I told Malachite it was over between us. I think that's when she went to the Grand Beacons. If I wasn't going to participate in her plot, she wanted me out of the way."

"What plot?" Jesse asked.

Jasper looked from left to right and moved a little closer to the grate, still without touching it. "Malachite is in league with dark forces," he whispered.

"Who?" Jesse and Daisy whispered back through the grate.

"I have never met them myself. All I know is that they are not of this realm. Malachite made a pact with them. In exchange for Emerald and a mother lode of precious gems, they said they would help her seize the Ruby Throne. She needed my help to get Emmy to stay here in the Fiery Realm. If I made Emmy claim me as her fiery mote, Malachite promised that she and I would share the Ruby Throne."

"Then I hate to say it," Daisy said, taking one step backward, "but the Beacons are right. You are a traitor."

"That's just it!" Jasper said. "I don't *want* the

Ruby Throne! I no longer even want Malachite. I really like Emerald! For the first time, I know what it's like to have a she-boon."

"So how did Malachite meet up with these dark forces?" Jesse wanted to know.

"She met them while patrolling the Outer Reaches," Jasper said. "She must have penetrated the membrane where it is thinnest, near the Great Grotto."

"What membrane?" Jesse asked.

"One of the membranes that lies between our realm and yours," Jasper said.

Jesse's eyes darted about. His mind was racing. "Daisy," he said, his voice charged, "do you think that membrane might be anywhere near where Queen Hap imprisoned St. George?"

"St. George!" Jasper burst out, his golden eyes gleaming in the dimness. "*That* was what she called him! The first time she heard his voice, it was coming from inside a block of amber."

Daisy said, "Tell us, would Malachite's flame be hot enough to melt the amber?"

Jasper nodded. "Malachite has one of the most powerful flames in the realm," he said.

"So St. George got Malachite to melt the amber and set him free!" Jesse said. "That's what Queen Hap meant by 'things heating up.'"

"And rumblings and tumblings," Daisy said. Her eyes met Jesse's. "Do you think the treasure St. George was searching for when he was digging in the hobgoblins' mine was actually in the Fiery Realm?" she asked.

"It makes sense," Jesse said. "I mean, the gems in this place would be worth gajillions to someone in the Earthly Realm."

"Plus it explains how Sadra escaped from the Toilet Glass," Daisy said. "St. George broke the spell and freed her! Who knows what powerful magic they can unleash together!"

"And now Emmy's gone looking for them both!" Jesse said. He pressed his face to the grate. "How do we get there, Jasper? Which way to the Outer Reaches? You've got to tell us. Emmy may be in great danger!"

Jasper wagged his head. "Sorry, Keepers. I've never been there myself. The fact is, I'm a bit of a homebody. I'm afraid I am worse than useless. Poor Emerald!"

Daisy said gently, "You've actually been a big help. At least we know what's going on. Now all we need is a plan!"

"Let's not make it here," Jesse said, standing back from the grate and brushing the flakes of rust from his forehead.

"Why not here?" Daisy said. "Maybe Jasper can help us."

Jesse leaned over and whispered in Daisy's ear, "Not here." He reached out and lightly tapped the rusty grate holding Jasper prisoner. "I'll tell you why as soon as we're out."

They bid Jasper a hasty farewell and followed the fire fairies out of the hole and back up the rusty winding stairs. Every time Daisy started to speak, Jesse shushed her.

Finally, when they had cleared the pink quartz gates of the Grand Hall, Jesse broke their silence. "Remember Lady Flamina said she could hear us coming on Old Bub because of the rusty horseshoes?"

Daisy nodded slowly as they walked.

"That's why she and Lord Feldspar allowed us to visit Jasper in the rusty hoosegow," Jesse said.

"I get it!" Daisy said, her eyes lighting up. "The *rust* helped them overhear everything we said!"

"Exactly!" Jesse said.

Daisy hesitated. "But that's good, isn't it?" she said. "Because Jasper's innocent, and now they've heard it for themselves and will set him free."

"Maybe," said Jesse. "But I don't think we can stick around to find out. We need to track down

Emmy." Jesse looked at the fire fairies. "We're going to the Great Grotto, guys," he told them.

The fire fairies sputtered.

"We have no idea how to get there," said Flicker.

"But we want to go with you," said Fiero.

"How can we help?" said Spark.

"Fiero and Flicker," said Daisy, "you go fetch Opal and Galena, and anyone who knows the way to the Great Grotto."

"Spark," Jesse said, "can you go to the stables to get Clipper and Speedy? We're going to need our trusty mounts."

The fire fairies dispersed to carry out their assignments.

When the Keepers got back to the cottage, Daisy said, "Let's check the Fire Screen. Who knows? Maybe Miss Alodie is sitting by the fire." Daisy waved her hand over the wall in their bedroom.

Sadie Huffington, otherwise known as Sadra the Witch of Uffington, appeared on the screen. The cousins yelped and jumped behind the computer table.

CHAPTER NINE

THE ORDER OF EMERALD

Sadra's wavy red hair and the sharp planes of her face showed vividly on the Fire Screen, illuminated by the flickering flame of a torch. Even in the half-light, they could see that her lipstick was gleaming red, her teeth were large and white, and her eyes shone an eerie yellowish green. She strode down a passageway that sparkled with gemstones.

"I wonder where she is," Jesse whispered to Daisy.

"Do you think it's the Great Grotto?" Daisy whispered back.

They didn't get a chance to find out, because the next moment, a shadow blotted out their view. Someone had licked in, whether on purpose or by accident they could only wonder.

Jesse waved his hand and closed the Fire Screen. "So much for that," he said.

"Who needs lava-vision?" Daisy said. "We have work to do. If we're going up against George and Sadra, we need to be properly outfitted."

Jesse watched as Daisy got busy weaving her hands over her body. She looked a little like one of those irritating street mimes, only who she was supposed to be or what she was supposed to be doing was a mystery to him—until she had finished, when both mysteries were solved.

"Ta-da!" Daisy said. She stood, battle-ready, in a suit of fine silver chain mail, with a breastplate, leg armor, boots, and a helmet.

"You look great," Jesse said with envy. "Show me how you did that."

"It's simple. All you do is picture in your mind

what you want to make and then sort of fiddle with your fingers—"

"Like a mime?" Jesse said.

"Exactly!" Daisy said.

Jesse remembered a suit of armor he had seen in the British Museum. It had belonged to a page of Henry II of England. He had liked the way it sheathed the body of the child-size mannequin in the showcase. It looked strong and sword-proof but sleek and lightweight at the same time. With his eyes half-closed and his fingers busily working, he envisioned this same suit of armor, dense but not too heavy, covering his own body. When he opened his eyes, he was wearing it.

"Awesome armor!" Daisy said.

Not bad, Jesse thought. But he still needed something more. He closed his eyes again, ran his hands down his chest, and created a white silken tunic. Emblazoned across the tunic was a bright green dragon with green eyes against a field of— what else?—purple socks!

"Brilliant!" said Daisy, and instantly whipped up one just like it for herself. "Okay, now we need the weapons to go along with the outfits," said Daisy.

Jesse felt uneasy. "Really? Weapons can be dangerous if you don't know how to use them."

"No worries," Daisy told him, already getting busy with her hands. "Remember how well I danced at the Fire Ball?"

Jesse nodded. "You were practically a prima ballerina."

"Well, Emmy explained to me when we were getting ready for the ball that the same magic that allows us to conjure these things also helps us use them like experts!"

Jesse thought quickly. "So I could make a guitar and play it like one of the Beatles if I wanted to?" he asked.

"Probably . . . But right now, it's weapons we need, not guitars."

Daisy made herself a sleek golden bow with a taut silver string. After that, she produced a quiver full of ebony arrows tipped with silver and fledged with the feathers of fire birds.

Not to be outdone, Jesse went ahead and fashioned himself a crystal sword with a silver handle studded with emeralds. The sword had two razor edges that tapered to a sharp point. Then he made a silver scabbard that hung low on his left hip so that he could reach over with his right hand and loose his sword.

Jesse went outside and held the sword high,

toward where the sun might be if there were such a thing in this place. "For the greater glory of Emerald of Leandra!" he cried.

"All hail Emerald!" Daisy shouted.

They began to test their skills with these new weapons. Jesse pranced around the garden, pretending to fend off a platoon of topaz sunflowers, slicing off head after head with speed and deftness. Daisy aimed at a faraway tree and brought down one ruby apple after another. When her quiver was empty, she snapped her fingers and more arrows appeared.

"Nifty," Jesse said. "You don't even have to retrieve your arrows."

"But you do need to put the heads back on Emmy's sunflowers," Daisy said.

Jesse smiled slyly. "Only if you put the apples back on that tree," he said.

"Deal," said Daisy.

They each went about repairing the damage they had done. Neither felt particularly elated about these new skills they had acquired. It was like being in possession of a magical loaded gun that could hit whatever you waved it at. Although they didn't say so, they both felt suddenly weighed down by a grave responsibility. It was not unlike how they had felt when they first learned they were

Dragon Keepers. Now, in order to defend the dragon in their keeping, they might have to shoot arrows into real hearts and lop off real heads.

"What I don't understand," Daisy said when she returned from sticking the apples back on the tree, "is why Emmy would just slip off by herself and not tell us where she was going."

"I was thinking about that—" Jesse began, but he was interrupted by the arrival of a gaggle of fire fairies and dragons.

Opal and Galena had brought someone they had met at the Beacons' runching, a medium-size she-dragon named Mica, as well as a couple of Jasper's boons, two blustering lugs named Citrine and Zircon. Fiero and Flicker had pulled together a ragtag assembly of their fellows. Bringing up the rear was Spark, leading the fire salamanders, Speedy and Clipper. Jesse was glad to see that Speedy's tail had grown back.

"Hold up a sec!" he said. He ran into the cottage and got the backpack, adjusting the straps so that it fit over his suit of armor. When he came outside, he saw that the dragons now wore tunics or breastplates emblazoned with the Emerald crest.

Daisy, who stood on the porch, clearly felt obliged to make a speech to their small crowd of supporters: "I want to thank you all for coming here this morning on behalf of Emerald and Jasper."

This brought forth a lively round of applause from the crowd.

"I believe you all know now of the threat to the Fiery Realm," Daisy continued, "by dark forces from the Earthly Realm, in the persons of Sadra the Witch and St. George."

The dragons nodded and the fire fairies flared brightly in response. Jesse was thinking that Daisy didn't sound like herself. She sounded like someone much older and more serious.

"St. George," Daisy said somberly, "is known to us in our world as St. George *the Dragon Slayer!*"

This set off a howl of outrage from the dragons. Daisy could not have gotten them more worked up had she suggested that they use chains of iron to jump rope.

"I don't need to tell you," said Daisy, telling them anyway, "that St. George the Dragon Slayer is your mortal enemy and must be stopped at all costs."

The dragons bellowed and stomped. The fire fairies, even rosy Fiero, went bright white with zeal. The fire salamanders, picking up on the general excitement, slapped their tails on the ground with a hollow thumping noise that sounded a little like war drums.

"Malachite thinks that St. George will help her gain the Ruby Throne, but my cousin and I have gone up against this man and we know this: the only person he ever helps is himself!"

The dragons and the fire fairies muttered darkly and shook their heads.

"We must expel St. George and his consort from the Fiery Realm and throw Malachite in the hole in place of Jasper."

"Yay, Jasper!"

"Booo, Malachite!"

When the noise had died away, Daisy said, "All right, who among you knows the way to the Great Grotto?"

The dragons and fire fairies looked uneasily at one another, as if each were waiting for one of the others to step forward and offer something useful.

Finally, the dragon named Citrine spoke up. "Only Malachite and her patrol have ventured that far into the Outer Reaches. And they disappeared last night."

Daisy groaned in disappointment. But Jesse didn't despair, because while Daisy had been making her speech, his eyes had been busy. He wondered why he hadn't seen it before, and he guessed that it was because he hadn't been looking for it. The moment he started looking for it, he saw it as clearly as the lines on the palm of his own hand.

"Um, Daze?" he said, tapping her on the shoulder. "Look down."

Daisy frowned in perplexity. "Why should I look down?"

"Just do it," he said, smiling. "Trust me."

Daisy looked down.

"What do you see?" he prompted her softly.

"I see a lava gym sock lying on the stairs," Daisy said with growing excitement.

"Look over there and tell me what you see," Jesse said, pointing to the lake path.

"I see more socks! Lots more socks! Once again, our dragon left us a trail of socks to follow!" Daisy said. "Let's get going!"

"For the greater glory of Emerald of Leandra, forward, ho!" Jesse cried.

Fiero, Flicker, and Spark led the way, following the trail of socks along the shores of the Lake of Fire. They set the pace for the salamanders carrying Jesse and Daisy, followed by the dragons on whose tails the other fire fairies—whose names were Cinder, Ember, Tinder, and Kindle—hitched a ride. In among the socks, there was a jumble of tracks that Zircon told them were the footprints of at least five dragons.

"Malachite and her rumble!" Daisy said. "Do you think Emmy was tracking them?"

"Either that or they were tracking her," Jesse said.

The spires of the Ruby City soon dropped behind them as jagged garnet bluffs rose up on their right. The Lake of Fire widened into something that looked and felt like the sea, with a ruler-straight shoreline. When they lost track of the socks, the jumble of dragon footprints led them onward. And whenever they began to feel light-headed and peckish, the fire fairies found crevasses with air fountains, where everyone took a turn runching on the oxygen bubbling in through the rocks from the Airy Realm. It was like the water fountain at school on a hot day after recess when you had to wait in line to get a drink.

Finally, they reached a point on the shore where both socks and tracks dwindled out. The fire fairies flitted up and down the shoreline, but their search was in vain because the trail clearly ended here. The last marks were two deep dragon footprints dug into the sand, with long gouges on either side.

Daisy frowned down at them. "This is where

Emmy popped her wings and took off," she concluded.

"Right," said Jesse. "But where to? And how are we supposed to follow?"

"In that, I think," said Daisy, pointing. It was difficult to see at first because it was made out of pinkish crystal and blended in. But by staring very hard at it, you could make out a vessel, like an oversize rowboat made from crystal, bobbing invitingly on the waves about thirty or forty yards from the shore.

"I wonder who it belongs to," Jesse said.

"Who knows?" said Daisy. "But finders keepers."

Everyone worked together to conjure up a couple of rafts sturdy enough to hold the weight of several dragons and a couple of fire salamanders. When the rafts were finished, Daisy and Jesse tried to coax the fire salamanders on board, but they hung back. They dug their feet into the sand. They brayed and wallowed. They spat wads of petulant fire that set off small explosions.

"I don't think they like the sea," Fiero said.

"What are we supposed to do now?" Jesse said. "We can't just abandon them here on the beach."

"Yes, we can," said Spark. "They'll find their way back to the stable."

So everyone piled onto the rafts, Citrine and Zircon pushing them with long poles out beyond the foamy pink breakers toward the ship. Daisy was happy to see Clipper and Speedy vamoosing down the beach toward the Ruby City like a pair of red-and-white barber poles on legs.

With help from the two biggest dragons, they all boarded the boat, distributing their weight evenly so that the vessel wouldn't list. Opal and Zircon stayed on the port side with Jesse and Daisy; Mica and Galena went over to the starboard side. Citrine remained amidships. The fire fairies crewed, flitting about the deck and the rigging, carrying out Citrine's orders.

"Weigh the anchor!" Citrine bellowed.

Spark and Fiero pulled up the anchor by its crystal chain.

"Hoist the mainsail!" Citrine shouted.

The fire fairies hauled up a sail of shimmering copper-colored silk, which immediately filled with the warm winds gusting from the shore and sent them whooshing out to sea.

The cousins stood at the rail and watched the foaming pink wake. Jesse pointed. "More socks," he said.

"She must have dropped them as she flew," Daisy said. "It's good to know we're headed in the right direction."

"This is kind of fun," Jesse said.

Just then, a head the size of their entire boat emerged from the sea. Covered in purple scales, it had yellow fangs, fiery red eyes, and a long plum-colored tongue. On a long, thick neck, the creature lifted its whole head out of the water, dripping and hissing and weaving. All hands shrank to the far side, and the deck tipped toward the sea, away from the long, slithering tongue.

Jesse drew his sword and scrambled up the pitched deck, prepared to do battle with the monster.

Opal caught him by the tunic and drew him back to her side. "Resheathe your weapon, Keeper," she said. "That creature's all spit and no flame."

As if it had heard, the monster reared back and spat, covering the ship from stem to stern in a great dripping glob of spit the color of grape bubble gum.

"Did I say this was fun?" Jesse said through a faceful of purple goo.

But the spit smelled familiar to Daisy, like the stuff in the canteen: hot and peppery one minute, cool and minty the next. It was sort of refreshing. "It's a fire serpent!" Daisy said.

"Right you are," said Opal. "This sea is its home."

As if hocking that humungous wad of spit had satisfied it, the fire serpent sank beneath the magma waves and disappeared from sight.

Everyone returned to their places. The fire fairies swabbed the decks and distributed silken cloths for the passengers to clean off the purple slime.

"I liked that stuff better from a canteen," said Jesse. He was just handing the soiled cloth to Flicker when Fiero, up in the rigging, called out: "Land ahead!"

They lined up along the port rail and looked. The shore they were nearing had a winding beach of glistening black stone. Just beyond the narrow beach, a jungle rose up like a long red wall of fire. Emmy had left a series of purple socks that led up the shingle and disappeared into the thick of the jungle.

"Prepare to drop anchor!" Citrine called out to the fire fairies.

They anchored just beyond the breakers, where they conjured up two more rafts to carry them to the shore. Stepping out on the beach, they gathered at the head of the trail. The jungle was dark and deep. Everyone stood around, peering uneasily into the tangle of trees. No one seemed particularly enthusiastic about entering it, even though the line of socks beckoned. The trail that led into the jungle was crude and narrow, the sort made by wild animals.

Jesse stepped away from the group, drew his sword, and held it high. In a voice slightly less robust than the one he had started the trip with, he cried out, "For the greater glory of Emerald of Leandra, forward, ho!"

"All hail Emerald!" everyone cried.

They fell silent as they entered the jungle. The trees were much taller than they had appeared from the beach, towering overhead as in a rainforest. The strange cries of birds and insects echoed in the warm pink fog, a fog that penetrated their clothing and worked its way into their lungs, sending them into fits of sneezing and coughing. It was like being in a vast steam room with a bunch of people with very bad colds. The footing grew soft and squishy, and the path narrowed.

Through the fog, Daisy saw trees and plants growing up out of pools of murky water. There were sections back home in the Deep Woods taken over by beavers that this place reminded her of, except that none of the growing things here were green.

Most were red. Many were black. It was creepy and unnatural.

Galena's voice came from somewhere behind them in the pink fog. "Whatever you do, Keepers, do not step off the path into the water."

"That's okay," Daisy assured her. "Jesse and I are good swimmers."

"Not here you aren't," Fiero said. "This whole area overlaps with the Watery Realm. That is the cause of the steam. Water is deadly to you now— as it is to us—and will remain so for as long as you reside in the Fiery Realm."

"Oh," said Daisy, and the hair on the back of her neck stood up. It was weird to think of the element that she had always considered a second home as being fatal.

Fiero lit on Daisy's shoulder. "I hate this place," she said with a flickering, sniffling shudder. Her jolly rosiness gone, she had shrunk down to a small blue knot of worry.

As Daisy walked along, the top of a scaly head poked out of one of the shallow pools just off to her right. It was greenish gray and let out a deep growl that set the water to bubbling and frothing. "Another fire serpent?" Daisy asked.

Fiero cowered behind Daisy's shoulder. "No!" she said timorously. "That is a water serpent. It is licking in from the Watery Realm the same way we lick in to the Earthly Realm. Usually, they don't let much more than their heads poke through. They're just curious. But I've heard of fire fairies getting extinguished by an accidental splash from a wet licker."

"Maybe *that's* what happened to the missing fire fairies," Jesse said. "They weren't kidnapped. They were just . . . accidentally extinguished by wet lickers."

"Never! Fire fairies would never come here on their own," Spark said.

After a while, the pools dried up and they were back on firm ground again. Everyone stopped sneezing and sniffling. Fiero gradually recovered her rosy glow and began bouncing about, pointing out the wildflowers and orchids to Daisy. Daisy took her wildflower notebook out of the backpack and sketched pictures of them as she walked along, writing down the names Fiero told her.

The jungle began to thin out, and eventually they emerged onto a rocky promontory. The view that stretched out before them took their breath away. For the longest time, they stood in silence, taking it in.

Finally, Fiero spoke up. "This is the Great Grotto. I have never been here myself, but my great-grandflame, Fiero the First, visited this place once and described it to me. I will never forget the stories she told."

"It's like the Grand Canyon," Jesse said, "only about twenty times bigger."

Dragons, Keepers, and fire fairies lined up along the rim of the canyon and continued to drink in the sight. The vast geological formation, extending off into the purple-pink mists, looked like an enormous multicolored geode, cracked open and lying before them. This place seemed to contain every precious and semiprecious gem in existence, mixed together like the colored sands of that other natural wonder, the Painted Desert.

"Got that spyglass handy?" Jesse asked.

Daisy conjured up another one and handed it to Jesse. He peered through it. "What do you make of that?" he asked as he handed the spyglass to her.

Daisy peered through it. A castle with stout turrets and soaring spires made of gleaming onyx clung to the side of the grotto, almost blending in with the natural onyx from which it had been hewn. Daisy didn't know what to make of it, but she did not like the look of it one bit.

"Is there a dragon or fire fairy settlement in the Outer Reaches?" she asked.

"No," said Opal. "This area is uninhabited."

"Not anymore, it isn't," said Daisy.

Then Jesse tugged at Daisy's arm. "Look up!" he urged her.

She trained the spyglass higher and then she saw it: a small green speck circling in the air above the castle. She brought the speck into focus until she saw two wings sprouting from it.

"That looks like our dragon!" she said happily.

"It sure is!" said Jesse. "We've always been on her back when she flew, and I never realized until now that her wings are purple on the top . . . but *green* on the underside."

Whether Emmy's wings were purple or green or, as was the case, purple *and* green, they were, by far, the most heartening sight Jesse and Daisy had seen in a long time.

CHAPTER TEN

THE CHAIN GANG

Everyone did their part. The fire fairies blazed their whitest and brightest. The dragons flamed for all they were worth. Jesse and Daisy conjured up a banner that read, HAIL, EMERALD! JESSE AND DAISY ARE OVER HERE!!!!!!

Their combined efforts paid off, because the speck began to enlarge as Emmy winged her way toward them. And then she was looming above them, her green scales shimmering. When she came in for a landing, everyone stood back to make way.

Dragons and fire fairies alike stood in awe of what did not exist anywhere in their realm: *a dragon with wings.*

Jesse and Daisy held themselves back while Emmy folded her wings against her body; then they ran and hurled themselves at her.

"We knew we'd catch up with you!" Daisy said.

"The old trail of socks," said Jesse. "Works every time."

"I'm very glad that it did," said Emmy. "I wasn't sure about lava socks. I was afraid the fire birds might eat them the way birds ate Hansel and Gretel's bread crumbs in the forest."

"Lucky for us, fire birds don't have a taste for socks," Daisy said happily.

Jesse stood back and tried not to sound too stern. "What made you go off half-cocked like that?" he asked.

"Oh, I was fully cocked after I visited Jasper in the pokey," Emmy said.

"How did you get down that spiral staircase?"

Daisy asked. "We barely fit down it ourselves."

"Plus it was made of iron," Jesse said.

"Those stairs are for fire fairies. I went in through the dragon's entrance, which is larger and iron-free," Emmy said. "I was heading back to my house when I spied Malachite and her rumble leaving the Ruby City. After Jasper spilled the peas to me about what they were up to, I just had to find out where they were going."

"Spilled the *beans,* you mean," said Jesse, grinning.

"Oh, no," said Emmy, with an adamant shake of her head. "It was peas. Peas, for sure. That would be P as in 'plot.' And P as in 'pee-yew,' that stinky George Skinner, stealing all the gemstones from the Great Grotto."

"So it's true," Jesse said. "St. George has escaped and is helping himself to the riches of the Fiery Realm."

"Sadra too, now," said Emmy. "Hop on my back and we'll go spying and catch the two of them purple-handed!"

"That's *red*-handed," said Jesse.

"Wrong again, Jesse Tiger! St. George and Sadra have *purple* hands now," Emmy said. "Purple gloves, purple coats, purple hoodies."

"Hmmm," said Jesse thoughtfully.

"Us too! Us too! We love to spy!" said Fiero, as she and Spark and Flicker all vibrated with excitement.

"Only if you promise not to tell the Grand Beacons I flew you," Emmy said.

"Cross our flames and hope to fizzle," all three of them vowed.

"Extraordinary times call for extraordinary measures," Jesse said. It was the thing Jesse's father said whenever the two of them got ice cream right before dinner.

Jesse and Daisy climbed onto Emmy's back. Then there came the familiar soft *pop-pop*ping sound as Emmy's wings unfurled to either side of them. The fire fairies scrambled onto Emmy's tail.

Emmy turned to the dragons and fire fairies remaining behind. "We'll make a full report when we come back. Meanwhile, why don't you fix us a cozy nest for the night?"

"Will do, Emerald," said Zircon and Opal, looking lively.

"Beware the Forces of Darkness," Galena intoned darkly.

"Yes, be very careful," said Opal as Emmy moved toward the edge of the precipice.

"Don't worry. I am a very careful dragon,"

Emmy assured them as she stepped off the edge of the grotto and into the air.

For a heart-stopping instant, Jesse felt himself falling as Emmy plummeted downward until, mere feet from the grotto's jagged garnet floor, her wings caught the updraft and she began to float, higher and higher. The fire fairies squealed in terror. Jesse knew just how they felt. The first time he flew on Emmy's back, he had been afraid, but the fear quickly vanished and was replaced by what he called the flying feeling, which was something like a wide-open singing sensation.

Before long, the fire fairies settled down as the grotto twinkled up at them like an enormous jeweled map. A sapphire plateau dropped down into a deep forest of emeralds, cut off by an arid stretch of topaz bordering an aquamarine expanse. Flying with Emmy made Jesse feel free, but it also made him braver, even as they flew straight toward the Onyx Castle, which grew out of the side of the grotto like a gleaming carbuncle.

Emmy swooped down low over the castle's ebony ramparts, close enough to see the flag flying from the highest spire, displaying the bloodred coat of arms of St. George the Dragon Slayer. If there was any doubt that St. George had staked a claim in the Fiery Realm, this dispelled it. Emmy glided deeper into the neck of the grotto that wrapped around the castle's base.

Daisy pointed out the line of gondolas below, the kind you see on freight trains carrying loads of coal. The hoppers were brimming with precious gems. A string of fire fairies, looking sad and blue, were loading the gems onto the gondolas. Behind his back, Jesse heard Fiero and Spark and Flicker muttering and sputtering with outrage.

"Hush, little ones," said Emmy in a low, urgent tone. "Dragon magic makes us invisible, but it doesn't muffle our sounds."

Spark, Flicker, and Fiero clung to Jesse and Daisy as Emmy drew near enough for them to see that the fire fairies were yoked together in a great gray web.

"Fire Banking Spell," Emmy whispered to the cousins. "Asbestos, actually."

Then there they were, the Forces of Darkness themselves, St. George and Sadra, lording it over the fire fairies. Either of these villains would have been quite frightening all by themselves, but together they nearly stilled the beating of Jesse's heart. Instead of the dragon skin dusters they usually wore, both St. George and Sadra were wearing long purple coats with hoods, high purple boots, and long purple gloves. Jesse guessed that these items had been made from the skin of a slain fire serpent, and he found himself wondering whether the serpent's skin was protecting them the way the serpent's Fiery Elixir had protected him and Daisy on their first day here, before their bodies had adapted.

Emmy stopped and hovered about five feet above and to the left of the hooded heads of St. George and Sadra. Jesse held his breath as St. George's head dropped back and he looked directly up at Jesse. St. George's eyes were golden, like his hair. St. George lifted an arm and pointed his gloved finger directly at Jesse, whose mouth went dry. Had Emmy's dragon magic been trumped by the power of the Slayer?

Then, in a voice as golden as his hair and eyes, St. George said, "There's some lapis lazuli up on that bluff. I want it."

"Then you shall have it, my prince," Sadra said, her voice taut with excitement and greed. "This grotto is all yours now."

Jesse looked where St. George had pointed. Sure enough, high above and behind him was a crag of blue stone. St. George had been looking *through* him at the stone. Emmy's magic had held. Against Emmy's back, Jesse sagged with relief.

Then Jesse noticed something very peculiar. George was holding something in his hand. Lime-green and shaped like an alligator, it was the kind of cheap water pistol you would find in a dime store. Sadra held one just like it, only hers was a hot-pink dolphin. The alligator and the dolphin were each attached by plastic tubing to white plastic cylinders strapped to St. George's and Sadra's backs.

This is nuts, Jesse thought. Just then, one of the fire fairies in the work crew stumbled and fell, scattering an armload of gems.

"Pick up your burden and keep moving!" Sadra snarled at it.

The fire fairy, obviously at the end of its strength, lay on the ground and moaned and thrashed.

Sadra pointed the plastic dolphin at the fire fairy. She squeezed the trigger and liquid shot out of the dolphin's mouth. Jesse almost laughed out loud. What were St. George and Sadra expecting to do? Soak the fire fairies into submission? But the laugh died in his throat, for the little fire fairy shuddered once and disappeared in a puff of steam.

A chorus of shrill screams erupted from the other fire fairies, but when Sadra aimed the pink dolphin at them, they shut up and started working at double time, picking gems off the grotto floor and loading them into the gondola bins.

Jesse held Spark, Flicker, and Fiero to his chest to keep them from throwing themselves at Sadra in a fit of white-hot fury.

Daisy hurtled forward and whispered in Emmy's ear, "Go! Go! Go!"

Emmy wheeled around and flew away over the grotto. The flight back was silent except for the steady *whoosh* of Emmy's wings. But no sooner had Emmy's feet set down on the grotto rim than the fire fairies hopped off her back to run and tell the others what they had seen.

In their absence, the other dragons had dragged large rough boulders into a circle. Over the boulders they had laid a row of long black fronds cut from the nearby jungle. It had the feel of a fortress more than a nest, which was just as well, considering what they had just witnessed. Zircon welcomed Emmy and showed her that he had situated their nest out of sight of the Onyx Castle and over a rift in the stones where there was an air fountain. That way, if someone got peckish in the middle of the night, he or she wouldn't have to wander from the nest to satisfy the need for a runch.

"Why did you use boulders?" Jesse asked. "Why not conjure up something more comfortable?"

"Safety is sometimes more important than comfort," Zircon explained. "The boulders are cordierite, which wards off evil spells as well as the wild fire beasts of the jungle."

Emmy and the Keepers needed some time to themselves, so they went for a walk along the grotto rim.

"Zircon is a very practical sort," Daisy said. "I like that in a dragon, don't you, Emmy?"

"Zircon is very nice," Emmy agreed.

"He's kind of dashing, too, don't you think?" Jesse said, taking his cue from Daisy. "He'd make someone's heart one great fiery mote."

"I like the dark-gray color of his scales. It's very distinguished, don't you think?" Daisy said.

Emmy narrowed her eyes, first at Daisy and then at Jesse. "I know what you two are up to," she told them. "Zircon is terrific, but Jasper is still the mote of my heart. The two of us are anything but splitsville."

Daisy exploded. "That big bronze galoot betrayed you!" she said. "He violated your trust!"

"That's true," Emmy said evenly.

"And broke your heart," Daisy added.

"It's mended now," Emmy said, making little stitching motions with her talons across her chest.

"How can you still love him?" Jesse said. "As far

as I'm concerned, he doesn't deserve your love."

"Keepers, I am touched by your concern. I know that Jasper lied to me at first," said Emmy carefully, "but in the end, he came clear."

"Came *clean,* you mean," said Jesse sullenly.

"No, Jesse Tiger," said Emmy. "It became crystal clear that he had undergone a change of heart about me."

"When did he change his heart?" said Jesse.

Emmy hesitated; then she said in a softer voice, "When he saw me with my Keepers and realized how we loved each other so."

Daisy felt a large lump forming in her throat.

Jesse's face colored bright pink.

Emmy went on. "You see, he had never felt anything like that love. He longed to experience it. I love you, Keepers, and I always will. The more love you give to me, and the more love I give to you, the more love I have inside me to give. There is plenty of love left in my heart to give to Jasper. And Jasper really needs it. It wasn't easy being Malachite's mote, you know. Once I have cleared Jasper's good name, he and I will find true happiness together."

"Just like Chamanda," said Jesse, looking all starry-eyed.

Daisy shoved him with one hand. "Jesse Tiger, what are you *talking* about?"

"Why, America's sweethearts, who else? Chad and Amanda!" Emmy said. "Otherwise known as Chamanda. Jasper and I are like that. What shall we call me and Jasper?"

"Let's see," said Jesse. "Emsper sounds kind of awkward. Jemmy? How about Jemmy?"

"Jemmy it is, now and forever!" said Emmy.

Daisy growled. "You two are talking tripe again." But she smiled all the same.

That night, after preparing a rustic runching courtesy of the air fountain, the dragons—Emmy, Mica, Zircon, Galena, Opal, and Citrine—arranged themselves inside the nest in a circle around the fire fairies: Fiero, Flicker, Spark, Cinder, Ember, Tinder, and Kindle. Jesse and Daisy nestled next to Emmy. It was then and there that Emmy and the Keepers delivered the complete report on their spying mission.

They confirmed to the group what Fiero, Flicker, and Spark had already let everyone know: that the Onyx Castle belonged to St. George and that he was the one who had been kidnapping and enslaving the fire fairies. He and Sadra were holding the fire fairies under a Fire Banking Spell, using them to set off explosions and loosen the gems from the grotto walls, then forcing them to load the loose gems into the gondola hoppers.

"So, Emmy, what's this about asbestos?" Jesse said.

At Jesse's words, the fire fairies and even the dragons shrank back and trembled.

Galena put their fears into words. "Folk of the Fiery Realm, dragons and fairies alike, are greatly weakened by this substance you named—asbestos," she said.

"So St. George imprisoned the fire fairies in a web of that nasty stuff?" Jesse said.

"That he did, Jesse Tiger," Emmy said.

"Villain!" said Flicker.

"Fiend!" said Opal.

"Stinker," said Emmy.

"Never mind all the name-calling," Daisy said. "Can you break the asbest—I mean, Fire Banking Spell, Emmy?"

"I might be able to," said Emmy carefully, "but it won't do much good if St. George and Sadra go and zap the fire fairies with tiny deadly plastic alligators and dolphins."

"I wonder what kind of evil stuff was in those pistols," Daisy said.

"The most evil of all substances in the Fiery Realm. More evil by far than asbestos," Fiero said. *"Water."*

CHAPTER ELEVEN

THE ONYX CASTLE

"I don't believe it!" said Galena, her pale-purple eyes going wide with shock.

"Monstrous!" said Opal, fanning herself with a black frond.

Meanwhile, all the fire fairies were flickering

174

and banging into each other like lightning bugs trapped in a small jar.

Daisy was astounded, until she remembered the lethal pools of water in the jungle. "So a squirt of plain old water was all it took to destroy that fire fairy?"

"As we have already told you, in the Earthly Realm, water will wet you," Fiero said. "But here, it extinguishes utterly. And now that you have adjusted to life here with us, it will have the same effect on you."

"You mean it would extinguish *us* utterly?" Daisy asked.

"Snuff you right out," said Spark.

"Which is why we need to come up with a plan," said Jesse.

Daisy blew her bangs off her forehead. "I wish somebody would tell me why St. George and Sadra are always so greedy!" she said. "Why can't they just go and rob a bunch of banks and leave well enough alone?"

"Who is Well Enough?" Emmy wanted to know.

"Us!" said Daisy.

Galena explained, "It's not a matter so much of greed for riches. It is greed for power. Gemstones are very powerful. Each stone holds within its sparkling facets a wondrous power. Whoever owns the gem possesses the power of the gem."

"What kind of power?" Daisy asked as she removed the notebook from the backpack and uncapped the pen.

"It depends upon the gem," said Opal. "Jade imparts wisdom; jasper—the gem, not the dragon—imparts relaxation; jadeite heals; and aquamarine aids in prophecy."

Galena joined in. "Garnet fosters inspiration and loyalty, emerald clairvoyance and insight, agate courage and strength, sapphire memory and performance in battle, bloodstone courage, ruby stability and help in opening portals."

"Which is why," Jesse said, "the Sorcerer's Sphere, which is a ruby, gets us into the Scriptorium!"

"Exactly!" Daisy said, looking up from her notebook, where she had been scrawling notes.

"There are many more gems," Opal said, "and they can all be found here in the Great Grotto. I could go on all night naming the gemstones and their powers."

Daisy looked eager to hear more, but Jesse said, "That's okay. I think we get the idea."

"With all these gems in their possession, they'll be more powerful than ever. They'll be able to do anything they want, anywhere they want to do it.

We really need to do something about this!" Daisy
said.

They sat around for a bit, brows wrinkled in
concentration, but the fact was that they were all a
little too tired to do very much in the way of con-
structive thinking. The fire fairies were already fast
asleep, their arms wrapped around each other in a
blue flickering heap in the center of the nest.

Emmy tilted her head back and cracked a wide
yawn. Emmy's yawn set off a chain reaction in the
other dragons.

If you have ever seen a dragon yawning, you
know that it is a sight only a Keeper could contem-
plate with comfort, for it involves a great many
teeth, a deep dark throat, and a long forked tongue.
Jesse and Daisy felt very much at ease here in this
nest, surrounded by yawning dragons. They were
just as exhausted, and so they crawled into their
warm slumber pouches.

"We'll sleep on it," Daisy said drowsily. "And
come up with a plan bright and early in the morning."

"Well, early, at least, if not exactly bright," Jesse
put in.

If any of them had any doubt as to how much
was at stake, Emmy took care of that at the exact
moment when everyone was just beginning to drop

off to sleep. Her words fell into the soft, reddish darkness like gold coins tossed into a well. "Whatever happens tomorrow, we cannot let St. George take the gemstones through the membrane to the Earthly Realm," she said.

"Of course not," said Zircon sleepily. "The gemstones belong in the Fiery Realm, on *our* side of the membrane."

"It's not just a question of *belonging*," said Emmy. "If the gemstones are transported through the membrane into the Earthly Realm, it will cause an imbalance in the way of things."

"Then what will happen?" Galena asked warily.

"I'm not sure," said Emmy, "but the effect will be cataclysmic . . . and it will spread to all of the realms: Earthly, Fiery, Airy, and Watery."

The silence was now downright tense.

Zircon was the next to break it. "Emmy?"

Emmy replied, "What is it, Zircon?"

"I don't understand. You're just a dragon— a dragon with beautiful purple-and-green wings, granted, but all the same . . . How is it you have come by such vital knowledge of the realms?"

Emmy heaved a sigh. "Beats me," she said. "All I know is that I know what I know. I don't always know *how* I know it. But I know that what I know is as true as truth can be."

"That's good enough for me," said Citrine behind a mammoth yawn.

"Thanks, Citrine," said Emmy.

When everyone had been quiet—and most likely asleep—for some time, Jesse reached out and squeezed Daisy's hand. "Tomorrow is Teachers' Conference Day," he whispered.

After a brief silence, Daisy whispered back: "We're on the eve of doing battle with the Forces of Darkness, and all you can think about is Teachers' Conference Day?"

"I can't help it. I *need* to think about stuff like that," Jesse said. "It keeps me from being too nervous. It helps me to know that somewhere, in some realm or other, somebody is leading a normal life . . . because we sure aren't."

"Yeah, well, we're the ones who wanted to go on magical adventures," Daisy reminded him.

"And now you have to pay the plumber," Emmy said.

"Pay the *piper,* you mean," Jesse said with a sleepy grin.

"No, Jesse Tiger, I mean plumber. I have been lying here thinking and thinking. When I was flying over the Onyx Castle, I saw pipes coming down from the castle into the cliff side. At first, I thought they were for poop and pee, but now I think the pipes lead through the membrane to the Earthly Realm."

"And that's why St. George conjured the castle over that exact spot!" Daisy said in an excited whisper. "They're going to bring the gemstones into the castle and flush them down the pipes into the Earthly Realm!"

"So if we take over the castle," said Jesse, "we can keep them from flushing the gemstones and save all the realms from devastating cataclysm!"

"Okay. Now that we've figured all that out, can we please get some sleep?" Daisy asked.

They woke up to another dark morning. After a bracing runching on air, there was the matter of equipment to attend to. Traditional armor and mail were of little use. This was a battle that called for only one thing: defensive rain gear. The castle was onyx, and so, to better blend in, they conjured in black. Every single member of their party made for themselves a complete set of slick black rain gear: coats and hats and boots and gloves and gaiters. To protect their faces, they wore black waterproof masks.

Jesse looked around at the black-clad dragons and fire fairies and thought that if the situation hadn't been so scary, it would have been ridiculous.

When they were finished, Emmy was the only one still standing around in her own green scales.

"Emmy," said Jesse impatiently. "Where's your gear?"

"Sorry, J.T., but black doesn't do a thing for me," she said. "Besides, haven't you heard? Green is the new black."

"Then wear *green* rain gear," Daisy said. "But please, *please* gear up like the rest of us."

Emmy screwed up her face in a way that reminded Daisy of when she was a baby dragon refusing to eat human baby food. "I don't like rainwear," Emmy said. "It'll make me look stupid and lumpy. Plus I'll get all sweaty and gross."

"Zircon's wearing a raincoat, and he doesn't look stupid and lumpy or sweaty or gross," Jesse said, although Zircon did look a little bit of all those things.

"And sweating is better than getting melted by a squirting plastic alligator or dolphin," Daisy added.

"I'll take my chances," said Emmy with a toss of her head.

Jesse opened his mouth to press their argument, but a warning look from Daisy told him to shut it.

"Suit yourself," Jesse said with a shrug.

"You mean *not* suit myself!" Emmy told him sweetly.

"*Whatever,*" Jesse growled.

On their way along the grotto ridge toward the Onyx Castle, the party passed through a patch of rich red bloodstone.

"Bloodstone gives courage," Galena reminded them.

"In that case, why don't we all choose a piece of bloodstone?" Opal suggested.

Jesse found himself a couple of bloodstones that were shaped like dice.

"See, Jess? Mine is shaped like an egg," Daisy said, showing him the one she had selected. Then she said to their dragon, "Where is your bloodstone, Emmy?"

"My heart is a bloodstone," Emmy said. She was preoccupied with the Onyx Castle, which loomed across the grotto from them. "Look, Keepers!" she said as she pointed to the set of railroad tracks that wound up to the castle.

"You were right, Emmy," said Daisy. "They're hauling the gems up to the castle."

"Right as grain," said Emmy.

"Rain," said Jesse.

"That, too," said Emmy with a canny nod.

Fortified with their bloodstones, the group forged ahead. From down below on the grotto floor, Jesse heard a series of small explosions: the band of captive fire fairies using their flames to blast loose the gemstones from the walls. The sound accompanied the group as they made their way around to the other side of the ridge.

The great gleaming black castle rose up before them. They stopped behind a row of onyx rubble and scanned the ramparts and the entryway. Jesse had expected to see Malachite and her rumble standing guard, but, just like yesterday, the ramparts were empty and the castle looked vacant and without defenses. What was more, the solid gold portcullis stood wide open and the drawbridge was down.

"It's like they were expecting company," Daisy whispered to Jesse through her waterproof mask.

"I don't like it," Jesse said. Beneath the rain gear, he felt the little flames on his arms and legs flaring up like a thousand warning signals.

Emmy apparently felt no such foreboding. She led them marching boldly across the drawbridge. No sooner had the last fire fairy passed beneath the gate than it came down with a crash, like the jaws of a giant trap snapping shut on them. At the same time, an earsplitting alarm went off. They staggered and jostled through the entryway, hands clamped over their ears. Water from unseen sprinkler heads bombarded them, pattering off their heavy-weather gear.

Daisy peered through the spray in search of Emmy. There she was, holding a giant purple umbrella, smiling. The alarm rose in pitch, and now sprinklers from the ground kicked up, too, hitting them from every angle.

"Emmy! Look out!" Daisy cried. What good would her umbrella do her now?

But Emmy calmly folded up her umbrella and tucked it under her arm. Far from melting, she danced and splashed in the spray like a kid running through a garden sprinkler. The alarm shut off. The spray died back and then cut off altogether.

"You're okay," said Jesse in the dripping silence.

"You see, Keepers? Not wearing the rain gear wasn't just a fashion statement," Emmy said. "I never even needed it in the first place." She splashed through a puddle. "Water doesn't melt me because I'm a lucky goose."

"*Duck,*" said Jesse. "It's lucky duck and silly goose. Of which you are both."

Zircon, who looked extremely uncomfortable in his lumpy rain gear, said, "Does that mean I can take this stuff off now?"

Emmy stopped splashing. "No, Zirky! I'm different. There are puddles everywhere, and you would perish the instant you disrobed. That goes for all of you. Keep your gear on!"

Jesse looked around. "I'm thinking that St. George and Sadra must have heard that alarm," he said.

"They'll probably be here any moment now," Daisy said.

"Then let's take to the ramparts," Emmy called out.

"For the greater glory of Emerald!" Jesse cried, and the others joined in.

"How embarrassing!" Emmy said.

They entered the castle and marched down flooded onyx halls, where the glossy black ceilings still dripped. The fairies, fearful of so much wetness even in their rain capes, perched on the shoulders of the dragons as the dragons sloshed up a flooded staircase. They poured forth onto a rampart, dragons, fire fairies, and Keepers arranging themselves along the crenellated wall facing the entrance to the courtyard. Inspired by Emmy, they now carried giant purple umbrellas as shields. They waited, elbow to elbow, in tense silence. It wasn't long before they heard a thundering on the drawbridge, followed by the creaking of the portcullis being raised. The small army on the rampart squeezed their bloodstones and braced themselves for battle.

"Wait until they're in the center of the court-yard to open fire!" Zircon said, passing the word down the line.

Moments later, Malachite and her rumble splashed into the courtyard wearing black water-proof jackboots up to their stout middles.

Malachite looked around.

"Hey, you! Malachite!" Emmy shouted down. "Up here!"

The great dragon's head jerked up, and then she smiled, as if the sight of Emmy made her day. "Emerald of Leandra!" she called out. "We meet again. I was hoping you would follow me here. For a powerful flying dragon, you are almost tiresomely predictable."

"Won't you be surprised," Emmy muttered under her breath.

"I see your Keepers have joined you, in spite of my efforts to hold them at bay," said Malachite.

"So *you* were the one who was blocking our view of the Fire Screen!" Jesse said.

"You probably stole the purple canteen, as well," Daisy added.

"Apparently, I should have done more," said Malachite. "I underestimated you."

"That's right," Jesse said. "We know everything. We know you've thrown your lot in with St. George and Sadra."

Malachite said, "And why shouldn't I?"

"Your father's going to be awfully disappointed in you," said Daisy with a wag of her head.

"I have been a disappointment to my father since the day I hatched. But I don't need his help or his approval anymore. With the help of my new boons St. George and his consort."

Daisy was just beginning to feel sorry for Malachite when Zircon roared, "Enough talk! We came here to fight, not talk! Fire when ready!"

"Give me your best!" Malachite replied. "I doubt it will be good enough."

Zircon belched a wave of flame that licked down the rampart, ran along the ground, and hissed at the feet of the rumble. Then the firestorm broke out, with the dragons on the rampart exchanging rounds with the rumble in the courtyard. All seven fire fairies flitted over the wall and came around behind the rumble, spitting small flames at them from behind and then dancing out of range of their swiping talons.

"Pssst," said Emmy, drawing Jesse and Daisy into the shelter of a turret.

"We're not flamers, so this is no place for us," Emmy said. "Let's go be plumbers!"

Jesse and Daisy followed Emmy back down the stairs and then down another set of stairs, all dripping water, leading into the basement of the castle. At the bottom of the stairs was the mouth of a pipe as big around as a water storage tank. Tracks across the basement floor led from a wide opening in the side of the castle into the massive pipe.

"Let's check it out, Keepers," said Emmy. "Maybe we can figure out a good way to block the pipe."

"When I was a toddler," Daisy said, "I used to throw my socks in the toilet and then push the flusher. I was little and didn't know any better. I thought it was fun. It used to clog the pipes and make everything back up and overflow, and my parents would have to call in the plumber. It happened a whole bunch of times, until I finally grew out of it. That's when Grandma started sending me the socks. It was to replace the ones I flushed."

"So that's how the sock tradition began," Jesse said. "I always wondered."

"Daisy, you are brilliant!" Emmy said. "I can conjure more socks and block the pipes, just like you used to when you were little. Come on! Let's go down the pipe and see what we can do."

The pipe might have been large enough to fit Emmy, but it still looked dark and creepy to Daisy. She shook her head vigorously. "Not me. You guys go," she said. "I'll stay here and stand guard."

Jesse hesitated. "Are you sure you're going to be okay here alone?" he asked.

"Better than I'd be with you guys down there," Daisy said with certainty.

"Okay," Jesse said, giving her a last worried look before disappearing behind Emmy into the mouth of the pipe.

Daisy took a look around. There was a wide square opening in the side of the castle, like a cargo bay in a warehouse or a picture window without any glass in it. She went to the edge of it and looked out. The tracks they had seen from across the way wound down to the bottom of the grotto. St. George and Sadra had hauled the gemstones up here on the tracks and then unloaded them and flushed them down the pipe. It was a long trip up from the bottom of the grotto to where she was standing.

Then Daisy heard the last sound she wanted to hear: the sound of a train of gondolas groaning and rattling up the tracks from the grotto below.

CHAPTER TWELVE

THE ETERNAL FLAME

Daisy's mind raced. She knew the rain gear and the umbrella were probably not going to offer enough of a defense against whatever was coming. She quickly conjured a suit of mail over her rain gear. She didn't care if she looked lumpy and ridiculous.

Wasn't it better to *be* smart and safe than to *look* smart and chic?

Daisy's thoughts jumped to weapons. The bow and arrows she had made for herself weren't going to do much good. The angle was too steep, and a bow and arrows were of no use in close combat. So she conjured up a sword like Jesse's. Next, she made a scabbard that hung low on her left hip so that she could reach over with her right hand and remove the sword in one smooth move.

Drawing her new weapon, Daisy kissed the blade and whispered, "For the greater glory of the Order of Emerald. All hail Emerald!" to give herself courage. Hilt braced in both hands, she positioned herself to one side of the bay and waited as the sound of the gondolas rattling up the side of the grotto grew louder with every passing moment.

Suddenly, four red-and-white-striped fire salamanders slithered into the room and looked around hungrily, as if someone had told them there would be food waiting for them at the top of the tracks. Hitched to the salamanders was the long train of gemstone-filled gondolas winding down the side of the grotto.

"Sorry, fellows, but you're about to lose your load," Daisy said as she hacked through the harness that bound the fire salamanders to the gondola train. The four freed salamanders immediately scuttled away.

The first car of the gondola teetered just below the lip of the bay. It was overflowing with sapphires that looked like pieces of a summer sky. Daisy resisted the temptation to run her fingers through them. Instead, she leaned against the car with her full weight and shoved. Gravity did the rest of the work as she stood back and watched.

The long train began to slide down the track, slowly at first, then faster, until the cars collided into each other. The train buckled off the rails. Cars crashed and spilled down the side of the grotto with a noise like an earthquake. Moments later, an enormous multicolored cloud of dust rose up and filled the air with swirling sparkles.

Daisy stood on the edge of the bay, her sword still drawn, and viewed with satisfaction the destruction she had, single-handedly, just wrought. And so easily, too! How she wished Emmy and Jesse had been there to see!

But Daisy's moment was short-lived, for the very next instant, Sadra leaped up into the bay. She was like a purple raptor, her red hair beneath the hood glittering with gem dust. Daisy backed away from her. She could almost *see* the fumes of fury rippling off the witch.

Sadra's yellow eyes narrowed. *"Why, you little witch!"* she whispered.

"Isn't that the cauldron calling the kettle black?" Daisy said, pleased at her cleverness in a pinch.

Eying Daisy's sword, Sadra conjured one of her own. "Yours is quartz. Mine is diamond!" Sadra informed her. "Nothing's harder or sharper than diamonds. That's why they're my favorite stone."

"For Emerald!" Daisy cried, lunging boldly at Sadra, but the witch parried with a slash of her diamond blade so swift that Daisy didn't even realize what had happened until she looked down and saw that the sleeve of her raincoat had been neatly sheared off, leaving her arm bare to the elbow. Luckily, it was her left arm, and she could hold it behind her back to protect it while she continued to fend off Sadra with the sword in her right hand.

"En garde!" Sadra cried triumphantly as she transformed her sword into a hot-pink dolphin-shaped water pistol.

"Touché!" Daisy countered immediately, turning her sword into a silver umbrella. Unfortunately, it was a closed umbrella. Infuriated, Daisy struggled to open it with one hand, but she needed both hands.

"This will teach you to meddle in the affairs of

those far greater than you, little girl!" Sadra cried as she let loose a powerful jet of water from the plastic dolphin's mouth.

Daisy felt an odd burning pain in her exposed left arm before it went completely numb.

Meanwhile, Emmy and Jesse had found the place where the pipe came flush against a long vertical crack in the onyx wall. It reminded Jesse of the crack in the wall at the bottom of the crater lake that had admitted them to the Fiery Realm on Friday. "This is it," he said to Emmy. "This is the membrane."

Emmy started to wedge lava socks into the crack in the wall. Jesse pitched in, and they were both working as fast as they could to stuff the crack when they heard Daisy scream. Jesse and Emmy stopped working and stared at each other. Daisy *never* screamed. They dropped their socks and tore back up the pipe toward the castle basement.

The first thing they saw was Sadra, standing halfway up the staircase, besieged by a ring of fire fairies. She was squirting them with the pink dolphin, but protected by their rain capes, they were plucking at her purple fire serpent coat and pulling off little pieces of it so that they could scorch the exposed flesh beneath. The witch was slapping at them, screeching in pain and anger. She dropped the pink dolphin and it clattered down the steps.

"Where's Daisy?" Jesse said, looking around.

He heard soft moaning, then he saw her, lying at the edge of the cargo bay looking so pale he barely recognized her at first. An umbrella with bent spokes lay on the floor next to her like a large black crow with broken wings. She was holding her left arm and slapping at it with her right.

"What's wrong, Daze?" Jesse asked.

"My arm's asleep," she said, continuing to slap it. "I can't get it to wake up."

"You mean you've got pins and needles?" Jesse asked.

"It's worse than that," Daisy said. "Sadra hit it with her water pistol and now it feels heavy . . . almost dead."

"You are lucky you didn't lose it. Oh, my poor dear Keeper!" Emmy cried out, scooping Daisy gently up in her arms.

"Make the feeling come back," Daisy said softly.

"Yeah," said Jesse. "Fix up her arm with dragon magic. Drown her in dragon tears and heal her the way you did yourself."

Emmy shook her head. "I wish I could. But dragon tears can't fix mortal wounds."

Jesse looked helplessly out at the grotto. "Then I'll get a mess of jadeite. How about that? Jadeite heals, right, Daze?" he asked his cousin, who looked so small lying in Emmy's arms.

Daisy nodded.

"Jadeite will only soothe her nerves," Emmy said softly. "It won't bring the feeling back in the arm."

"You mean my arm's going to stay dead?" Daisy asked.

Emmy nodded.

Jesse heard a wailing sound and realized it was his own voice. How was Daisy going to play sports? How was Daisy going to swim? How was Daisy going to get dressed in the morning? This was one magical adventure that had taken a truly sorry turn.

He felt someone tugging at the sleeve of his raincoat and turned to find Spark, Flicker, Fiero, and their four fire fairy friends standing in a timid half circle.

Jesse finally got a grip. "What happened to the witch?" he asked, looking around.

"We drove the fiery-haired one up into the courtyard and passed her along to Opal and Galena. It's their turn to have a little fun with the fearsome old hag," Fiero said.

Jesse saw that the fire fairies were holding

gems in their arms. "What's all this?" he asked.

"You said you needed jadeite," Flicker said timidly.

"We got a whole bunch for you," said Fiero.

"Aw, thanks, you guys," said Daisy softly.

"We found it outside, scattered down the side of the grotto," Spark said. "So we didn't have to go very far at all to find quite a bit of it."

"It must have spilled out of the crashed train," Jesse said.

"Our brave Daisy's doing," said Emmy proudly.

The fire fairies crowded around and gently packed the jadeite onto Daisy's inert arm. Daisy lay back and closed her eyes, the color beginning to return to her face. "I still don't have any feeling in it," she said. "But I do feel better."

"We never should have left her alone," Jesse said to Emmy.

"Are you kidding?" Daisy said. She sat up in Emmy's arms and brushed the hair from her eyes with her good arm. "I did a great job. I unhitched the team of fire salamanders that were pulling a whole trainload of gemstones up the side of the grotto. I shoved the cars and they went smashing and crashing down into the grotto. You should have seen Sadra! She was hopping mad. And I did it all by myself, single-handed." Daisy's face froze on the phrase "single-handed." Then she lay back down in Emmy's arms with a grim and unsettled look. "You should have seen me," she added with quiet dignity.

"There, there, my sweet Daisy Flower," said Emmy soothingly. "Courage needs no witnesses."

Jesse ventured a smile. "Way to go, Daze. You saved the realms."

"Daisy is so brave she deserves the Purple Star," Emmy said.

It was the Purple *Heart* and the *Silver* Star, but Jesse didn't have the stomach to quibble with Emmy just then.

"I wish I could say that the battle is over and done with," Emmy said sadly, "but there is still the Slayer to contend with."

"You guys stay here and guard Daisy," Jesse said to the fire fairies. "Emmy and I will go and hunt down St. George."

"Forget it!" Daisy said, rearing up and hopping down from Emmy's lap. "I don't need any guarding, and I'm not missing out on the hunt. You can count me in."

"Are you sure you're okay?" Jesse asked.

Daisy set her chin. "I'll be fine!" she said.

As their party emerged from the basement into the courtyard, they saw that the two sides were exchanging fire volleys there. Daisy counted heads.

Two of the four rumblers were missing in action.

Daisy turned to Fiero, who hovered protectively to her left. "Malachite's down two. What happened to them?" she asked.

Fiero pointed to some heaps of sodden ashes over by one wall. "They have merged with the Eternal Flame," she said.

"Unfortunately, the third heap is our own dear Mica," Flicker added sadly.

Citrine lay behind a pile of boulders in a corner of the courtyard. He was badly wounded and squeezing out tears to treat the burns. Zircon, exchanging pale rounds of flame with Malachite, looked done in. The good news was that Galena and Opal had pinned Sadra to the wall and weren't letting her go anywhere.

Emmy came up behind Zircon and tapped him on the shoulder. "I'll take over. You rest," she told him.

Zircon, nodding, staggered off to join Citrine. Jesse said to the fire fairies, "Go over there and protect those two while they catch their breath."

"Good idea," said Daisy.

The fire fairies, except for Fiero, who stayed with Daisy, swarmed over to hover around the two wounded and spent dragons. Meanwhile, Malachite looked as strong and ornery as ever. Daisy was afraid for Emmy, up against a fighting machine like this.

Malachite opened her mouth and flamed Emmy. Emmy held up her arm and the flames bounced off her. Daisy looked at Jesse, her eyes wide. Jesse whistled in amazement. The last time Emmy had been flamed, it had scorched her scales and driven her from the Fire Ball. Had she somehow developed a resistance to flame just as she had found a way to repel water? What a dragon!

"I'll tell you what, Malachite," Emmy said fearlessly. "I won't fly and you won't flame. That way, we're even."

"Agreed," said Malachite.

"Choose your weapon," Emmy said.

Malachite conjured up a club. It was a nasty-looking, knobby, petrified-wood thing, the kind of club that Daisy imagined cavemen fought with.

"All right," said Emmy. "If that's the way you want to play it." And so saying, Emmy produced her own caveman club.

The two dragons circled each other. Malachite swung her club at Emmy's legs. Emmy jumped in the air and the club whistled beneath her. Emmy swung her club and the blow glanced off Malachite's arm. Malachite worked her shoulder in the joint, then switched her club to her other arm and brought it crashing down toward Emmy's head. But Emmy ducked to the side and the club clipped her shoulder instead. Emmy swung her club at Malachite's head, but Malachite blocked it. The clubs cracked together, and then Emmy and her foe were going at it, club to club—*crack! crack! crack!*—until Emmy broke the rhythm by coming at Malachite hard from the other direction and knocking the club from her grip. The club went flying across the courtyard and bounced off a wall.

"Trounce her while she's unarmed!" Zircon shouted.

"Now's your chance!" hollered Citrine.

But Emmy, fair-minded as ever, lowered her club and gave Malachite a chance to rearm herself. As she went to fetch her club, Malachite had a crafty look in her eyes and Daisy wanted to cry out a warning, but her tongue felt glued to the roof of her mouth.

On the way back to Emmy, Malachite stumbled. Emmy reached out to steady her, and Malachite jammed the end of her club into the side of Emmy's head. Emmy staggered backward and fell down hard on her tail, the club rolling out of her grasp.

Malachite loomed over Emmy, a wide smile spread across her face. She lifted her club over her head. Daisy gasped and grabbed for Jesse's arm, but Jesse wasn't there. She looked around frantically. Fiero flicked Daisy on the shoulder and pointed.

Jesse was leaning over the rampart directly above Malachite. In his hands was a wobbly black balloon filled with water. Malachite was just bringing the club over her shoulder to clobber Emmy when Jesse released the water balloon. The balloon landed on the point of Malachite's centermost horn and burst. Water exploded all over the dragon, dissolving her as instantly as sugar in a pot of boiling water. Daisy heard Jesse's loud whoop of triumph and then his footsteps, coming rapidly down the stairs. He dashed into the courtyard just as Emmy was climbing shakily to her feet.

"Good shot, Jesse Tiger!" Emmy said.

"Ah! Emerald! Rallying just in time for your rather overdue slaying!"

Jesse's glance flew up to the rampart. There was St. George. His hood was down and his golden hair gleamed against the dark sky.

"He's unarmed," Daisy said in a wondering voice.

"He only *looks* that way," Emmy said. "I'll believe that when wild boars fly."

"Pigs," Jesse whispered as Emmy flew up and alighted on the wall of the rampart directly across from St. George. "Why don't you come over here and fight me, Georgy Porgy?"

"I'd much rather stay here, Emmy-wemmy," said George mockingly, "and blast you to the Eternal Flame." He waved toward the turret.

Jesse heard something heavy grinding across the stones. A moment later, a cannon rolled into view, pushed by an invisible force.

"How do you like my new toy?" said St. George, beaming with evil glee.

"Cannons aren't toys," Emmy said, frowning.

"Oh, but this is a very special toy," he went on, resting the barrel in an indentation in the crenellated wall. "This, my poor, naïve, thoroughly *inadequate* draconian foe, is what is called a *water* cannon."

A cry of distress rose up from the dragons in the courtyard. The fire fairies keened.

"Haven't you heard?" Emmy called across the space between them. "Water can't hurt me."

"Ah! But it can hurt all those snivelers down below!" he said, gesturing to the courtyard, where Zircon and Citrine, Opal and Galena, Jesse and Daisy, the last two rumblers, and all the fire fairies looked fearfully on. "It can hurt all your loved ones. It can hurt your Keepers most especially and quite terminally, I am pleased to say."

"No, it can't. Can't you see, you arrogant fool?" Emmy said in proud defiance. "Those black coats they are wearing are waterproof. Your cannon can't hurt them."

St. George cracked a crooked smile. "Ah, but it can, you see. The water will be propelled from this cannon with such force that it will blast the rain gear from their bodies, soak them to the skin, and then melt them to mush."

Emmy was silent. Jesse thought that he saw her confidence flag for the first time.

Suddenly, they heard a loud pounding sound. Someone was crossing the drawbridge!

The next moment, Jasper came barreling into the courtyard. He looked around and called out, "Emmy! Where are you?"

"I'm up here, Jasper!" Emmy cried out eagerly.

Jasper turned and looked up. "There you are!" he said. "I thought I'd never see you again. The Beacons declared me innocent and freed me from the hole. I followed your trail."

"I'm very happy to see you, Jasper, my dear mote," Emmy said cautiously, "but I'm afraid it's not safe for you here."

Jasper turned and looked up at the other rampart. "You must be St. George!" he said.

"Yes," St. George drawled, "the agent himself."

"The agent?" Jasper asked.

"Why, the agent of your destruction!" St. George cried out, firing the water cannon. The water roared from the barrel and hit Jasper dead on. All that remained of the dragon when the cannon stopped firing was a pile of bronze-colored goo.

"No!" Emmy let out an agonized scream. *"Not Jasper!"*

Jasper had merged with the Great Flame.

CHAPTER THIRTEEN

THE PURPLE STAR

St. George patted the cannon's barrel. "Let me see," he said, pretending to study the crowd down below, gloved finger to his lips. "Who shall I melt next? One of the Keepers, I think, but which one, is the question. The boy, I think. Let the girl suffer as a one-armed wonder for a while longer before I finish her off. Yes, the boy . . ."

St. George swung the cannon around and brought it to bear on Jesse. Jesse swallowed hard.

"No!" Emmy howled again. *"Not my Keepers! Never!"*

Emmy flung back her head and opened her mouth. A howling wind blew forth from it. It blew everyone else clean off their feet and pushed them against the far wall of the courtyard. Jesse managed to cling to a post with one hand and to Daisy's hand with the other. Daisy hung on to Jesse, her body flying parallel to the ground, like a black flag rippling in a high wind.

"Are you okay?" he called out to her over the roaring wind.

"I'll be fine!" she shouted back.

Jesse looked up and saw George gripping the barrel of the cannon while the wind from Emmy's mouth tore the purple coat right off his back.

"Look, Daze!" he shouted to her.

The purple coat blew away, leaving the long black coat, the one made from Balthazaar's skin. But even that magical dragon-skin garment failed to withstand the power of Emmy's blast. The coat blew off into the grotto, leaving St. George in a pair of long black underwear. Finally, Emmy closed her mouth and cut short the windy onslaught.

Just as Daisy's feet touched the ground again, Emmy took another deep breath and opened her mouth anew. This time, fire blasted out, a bright orange with tongues of red and yellow and even purple and green.

It was a glorious fire, a scathing fire. It licked across the space of the courtyard and knocked St. George right off the rampart.

"Our winged dragon can *flame*, Jess!" Daisy said, flapping her good hand with joy.

Meanwhile, Emmy had turned her attention to the last two rumblers.

"We'll be your boons now!" the two of them said, ducking their heads behind their paws. "We promise."

Emmy nodded, satisfied. Then she looked at Sadra, cowering against the wall behind the two she-dragons.

"But this one here can make no such promise. Stand aside, boons!" Emmy shouted.

Opal and Galena fell back. Sadra, her tattered purple coat flapping about her ankles, made a run for it across the courtyard toward the exit.

Emmy opened her mouth and aimed a fresh flame at Sadra's feet. The witch went screaming and yelping and hopping over the drawbridge and out of sight.

Emmy closed her mouth and stanched the flame.

"Jesse Tiger!" she called out a trifle hoarsely.

"Yes, my magnificent fire-breathing Emmy?" Jesse replied.

"Go and see if you can find the black coat," she told him.

"Balthazaar is going to be one happy dragon," Daisy said.

Emmy unfurled her great purple-green wings and lifted off the rampart.

"Where are you going?" Jesse and Daisy called out to her.

"I'm going to finish what I started," she said with a fierce look in her emerald eyes. "First I'm going to break the Fire Banking Spell and free the fire fairies down at the bottom of the grotto. Then I'm going to deep-six that dastardly duo."

"What did you do with St. George and Sadra?" Daisy asked as soon as Emmy returned to the castle, leading the jubilant band of liberated fire fairies up from the grotto below.

"First of all, I flew them back to the Earthly

Realm. Next of all, I imprisoned them in the biggest, stinkiest conch shell I could find," Emmy said with grim satisfaction. "And last of all, I dropped that conch shell down to the bottom of the Mariana Trench."

"What's that?" Daisy asked.

"It's in the Pacific Ocean," Jesse said with a grin. "It's the deepest and darkest of the deep dark undersea canyons. Perfect."

"That's what *I* thought," said Emmy.

These were the last words Emmy would speak for the whole trip back to the Ruby City.

To show their gratitude to Emmy for rescuing their captive fellows, the fire fairies gathered up the ashes of Jasper and placed them in a box carved from jasper stone. It was shaped like a child's chair, with a trapdoor seat, beneath which the ashes lay.

"What is it?" Jesse asked Fiero.

"It's Jasper's Eternal Throne. It will be placed in the Hall of the Eternal Flame, where all the other dragons of this realm rest. We are all Grand Beacons in the Hall of the Eternal Flame."

Emmy carried the throne on the trip back to the Ruby City and never let it out of her sight.

The odd thing, Jesse found, was that their dragon didn't weep. Perhaps if she had, he and Daisy would have been able to comfort her. They were used to Emmy crying. They knew how to dry her tears, how to croon to her, and, after the storm of tears abated, she always felt better. But this was different. Daisy's lifeless arm and Jasper's lost life had plunged Emmy into deep gloom, removing her to a place where not even her Keepers could reach her.

Daisy was another matter entirely. Jesse had made the mistake of offering to carry the backpack, which was heavier than usual because the dragon skin coat was squashed into it.

Daisy turned beet red. "Let's just get something straight right now, Jesse Tiger! Number one: it's my left arm that's useless, and I happen to be right-handed. Number two: I am far from helpless. Number three: I can still take my turn carrying the backpack. I can do lots of things, just like before. I don't want your pity and I don't want to be coddled or treated like an invalid. If this is the way it's going to be from now on, I can get used to it. And if I can, you can! *I'll be fine!*" she added for good measure as she shrugged the hefty backpack onto her shoulders.

They returned along the same route they had come, by foot and then by crystal boat across the sea. As is so often the case, the journey back seemed to go much faster than the journey out. It was, however, a very *different* journey. For one thing, Emmy was with them, and for another, there were ten times as many fire fairies. But it was, in spite of their victory, a far less joyous group. For all that they had triumphed over the Forces of Darkness, they had done so at great cost. They had lost Jasper and Mica and Malachite and half her rumble, and then there was the matter of Daisy's arm.

At one point, Jesse finally got up the courage to ask the question that had been burning a hole in his tongue. "What are we going to tell Aunt Maggie and Uncle Joe when we get back to Goldmine City?"

"About what?" Daisy asked.

"You know . . . about your, uh, dead arm," Jesse said.

Daisy sighed. "That. I'll think of something, don't worry. Don't I always come up with the perfect cover story?"

True, Jesse thought. Daisy was very inventive when it came to cover stories. Still, losing a homework assignment was one thing, losing the use of an entire arm was quite another.

Some of the fire fairies had flitted ahead to let the Grand Beacons know what had transpired in the Outer Reaches. By the time they arrived at Emmy's cottage, there was a large crowd of dragons and fire fairies waiting for them.

Emmy's shoulders sagged at the sight of the welcoming committee. Clearly, all she wanted to do was climb into her crate and cradle Jasper's Eternal Throne to her breast. But being a hero comes with a certain obligation to celebrate and be celebrated. The Grand Beacons sent an honor guard to escort Jesse and Daisy and Emmy to the Great Hall of the Grand Beacons. Emmy and her Keepers had no choice but to go.

"Can I conjure you up a celebratory tiara or something?" Daisy asked Emmy.

Emmy shook her head and hugged the casket to her chest all the more tightly.

Daisy cast a look at Jesse. At the start of their trip back to the Ruby City, they had shucked off the rain gear and the suits of mail. They were once more clad in their Goldmine City clothes, their jeans and T-shirts and winter coats. "What about you, Jess?" she asked. "Can I whomp you up some fancy duds for the occasion? It ought to be red carpet all the way."

Jesse held up his hands. "Hey, I'm good."

"Don't you want to look glamorous?" Daisy asked.

"I'd rather be a bowwow than a wow-wow, I guess," he said listlessly.

"What's the matter with you people?" Daisy

said as she conjured herself up a deep-green velvet dress with matching shoes. The dress had long sleeves and a lace collar and cuffs.

"How do I look?" she asked Jesse.

Beautiful, Jesse thought, *except for the arm swinging uselessly at your side.* "You look great," he told her.

A parade of dragons and fire fairies followed the honor guards, the Keepers, and Emmy along the diamond path, beneath the city gates, and down the main boulevard leading to the Great Hall. The giant crystal sleighs chimed at them in greeting as they jostled past, the flame fairy passengers crackling and cheering. Dragons on the street stopped and bowed their horned heads in solemn recognition. The pink quartz gates of the Great Hall stood wide open, and the towering guards lined up and saluted them as they passed down the long red hallway, with Spark, Fiero, and Flicker darting along behind them.

Just before they entered the throne room, Daisy turned to Emmy and said, "Leave this to us. We'll do all the talking."

Emmy shrugged, as if talking had been the last thing on her mind.

Lady Flamina leaned forward attentively, while

Lord Feldspar sagged, his head bowed, tears dripping down.

Daisy whispered to Emmy, "Is Lord Feldspar crying?"

Emmy nodded. "Malachite *was* his daughter."

"I wonder if he suspected she was a traitor," Jesse whispered.

"Shhh," said Daisy, for the Grand Beacons were preparing to speak.

"The great tidings have preceded you," said Lady Flamina, burning mild and blue with an orange peak on the crown of her head. "You have rescued the kidnapped fire fairies and saved the realm from the depredations of the Forces of Darkness."

"I shall mourn the loss of my daughter evermore," Lord Feldspar grumbled. "I blame myself. I was too hard on her. I expected too much, and because of this, I placed the realm in great jeopardy." He shook his mighty head and looked down at the Keepers. "Tell us how it went in the Outer Reaches."

Jesse wasn't about to stand there and describe to Lord Feldspar how he had disappeared his daughter with a water balloon, so he said, "If it's all the same to you guys, we'd just as soon 'desist with the dithering details' and be on our way. It's Monday night. Teachers' Conference Day is over, and we have to get home. We have school tomorrow."

"And we're taking our dragon with us," Daisy emphasized for good measure.

When neither Beacon responded, Daisy added, "I mean, after what she did to defend your realm, we figure the least you can do is grant her leave."

Instead of striking them with lightning bolts of raging fury, both Lady Flamina and Lord Feldspar remained saddened and subdued.

"We agree with you wholeheartedly. It is the very least we can do," Lord Feldspar said. "In fact, in recognition of your service to the Ruby Throne, Emerald, we should like to bestow upon you the title of Ambassador to the Fiery Realm."

Emmy, still clutching Jasper's casket to her breast, said, "What's *that* mean?"

"It means," said Lady Flamina, her flame flickering bright gold with pleasure, "that you may move unimpeded between the two realms from this time forth."

"Thank you!" said Daisy, sagging with relief against Jesse's shoulder.

"What is more," Lady Flamina went on, "you may maintain title to your cottage on the shores of the Lake of Fire, and anytime you wish, you may return to visit. Each and every time, you will be greeted with the warmest of Welcoming Flames."

"Okeydokey, Princess Smoky," Emmy said.

The cousins shot startled looks at Emmy. Either she was beginning to perk up or she had lost her dragon marbles.

Undaunted by her new nickname, Lady Flamina continued. "As for the Keepers . . ."

Jesse and Daisy smiled wanly.

Lord Feldspar said, "We have a small token of our gratitude for the hand you played in this exploit and," he added sadly, his eyes on Daisy, "the arm whose use you seem to have . . . lost."

Daisy's ears, through her fair blond hair, turned hot pink.

"We are sorry indeed for your loss," said Lady Flamina to Daisy.

"I'll. Be. Fine!" Daisy said with icy precision.

An honor guard marched into the throne room. He approached Daisy first. When he stepped away, Daisy was wearing an amethyst pin in the shape of a star. Then he pinned Jesse with a dark blue ribbon that had a small silver heart dangling from it. For a moment, he was sorry he wasn't wearing the gaudy Las Vegas suit to go along with it.

"The Purple Star and the Silver Heart of the Grand Order of the Beacons," Lord Feldspar said grandly. "You are hereby honorary members of the Aura."

"Wowee-zowie," said Jesse.

Daisy dipped in a one-armed curtsey and smiled regally.

The Grand Beacons turned to Emmy. "And now, perhaps saddest of all is the fact that our own Jasper, the fiery mote of your heart, has merged with the Eternal Flame. We grant you the right to carry his Eternal Throne with you to the Earthly Realm . . . without bringing about dire consequences to the order of things."

"That's good," muttered Emmy to the cousins, "because I was going to bring him home with me anyway. And by the way, I'd like to go home now."

Home. Jesse lit upon the word with a sense of deep satisfaction. *Emmy is coming home.*

Then Lady Flamina and Lord Feldspar walked Jesse and Daisy and Emmy down the hall, through the streets, past the gates, and over to the banks of the Fiery Lake. They stopped more or less where Jesse and Daisy had stood when they first saw Emmy, so happy and carefree, running toward them down the beach with Jasper.

"This is where we say farewell," said Lord Feldspar. A large crowd of Fire Fairies and dragons had gathered on the shore.

"All you need to do to get home to the Earthly Realm is dive into the Lake of Fire and swim. Then scale the wall and go back through the membrane through which you entered," Lady Flamina said.

"Simple as that sounds," Daisy said, "I haven't learned to swim or scale one-armed yet, so I think we'll *fly* to the membrane."

"An exception to the rules is noted, and your request is hereby approved," said Lord Feldspar.

The cousins took a moment to say goodbye to Opal and Galena, to Zircon and Citrine, to Cinder, Ember, Tinder, and Kindle, and last of all, to their special new friends, Spark, Fiero, and Flicker.

"Think of us the next time you look into a fire," said Flicker.

"Who knows?" said Fiero, an impish gleam in her eyes. "You might even see me licking through."

"You always do all the licking," said Spark, flaring up.

"Yeah," said Flicker. "No fair!"

And before long, the three fire fairies were arguing, noisy as a pack of firecrackers going off on the Fourth of July. Jesse and Daisy left them to it and climbed onto Emmy's back.

"Hold Jasper for me, will you?" said Emmy, handing the throne back to Jesse. It was heavy, but Jesse didn't want to ask Daisy for help, given that she had only one good arm. Then Emmy popped open her wings, and the vast assembly of fire dragons and fairies ranged along the lake cheered at the magnificent sight of the purple-and-green dragon wings. Emmy took flight and soared out over the Lake of Fire. She flew one circle around the group below, giving them a chance to admire her wings and to wave their final farewells. Then she flew straight toward the crack in the cliff. Jesse was just beginning to worry about how Emmy was going to land on the narrow ledge when the crack in the rock opened up.

"Hang on tight," said Emmy as the magma closed around them.

Jesse and Daisy clung to Emmy as she began the upward swim through the thick, warm ooze.

Chapter Fourteen

FIRE ARM

It was early Monday evening when they emerged from the crater lake and clambered up on its banks. It was the same time of day it had been when they left the Earthly Realm on Friday. The sun was turning the surface of the lake a deep pink that reminded Daisy of the color of the sky in the Fiery Realm. She knelt down and dipped her hand into the water. It was icy cold. She pulled her hand back. Her fingers tingled.

"Well, I guess that's that," she said, standing up. She shook out her hand, but the tingling didn't go away. She laughed shortly. "Maybe I should tell my parents that I dipped my arm in the crater lake and froze it stiff."

Jesse was staring at her as if he had just seen a ghost, which, in a sense, he had. "Your arm!" he said, pointing.

"Yeah. Trust me, that water's freezing," said Daisy. "Knowing how you feel about cold water, I wouldn't advise you to go anywhere near it yourself, Jess."

"But you touched it with your *left* hand," Jesse said. "Daisy, *your whole left arm is moving!*"

Daisy looked down slowly. The left sleeve of her winter coat was no longer hanging limp and useless at her side. Her left hand was alive and well and shaking off the freezing-cold water.

"My arm got its feeling back!" Daisy shouted.

"Yay!" Emmy shouted. "Daisy has two good arms again!"

"Whoopee!" Jesse sang.

Jesse, Daisy, and Emmy did the Happy Prospector's Dance on the banks of the crater lake.

After a round or two, Emmy stopped. "Wait just a rootin'-snootin' minute here," she said.

Jesse was only too happy to correct her. "That would be rootin'-*tootin*'."

"Oh, no!" Emmy tapped the side of her snout. "Because it's my dragon *snoot* that tells me you might be on to something with this arm of yours, Daisy Flower. If damage that was done in the Fiery Realm was undone here, then maybe . . ."

Emmy lifted up the casket that contained Jasper's essence and removed the lid. They watched as she scattered Jasper's ashes over the water. The dust swirled out over the lake like a twinkling bronze fog.

Daisy was thinking, *How touching that she's spreading Jasper's ashes over the lake like that.*

Jesse was thinking, *Maybe now she won't be lugging that gloomy old casket around with her all the time.*

The next moment, Jasper's bronze, horned head poked out of the water. "Emerald!" he called out. "I'm back!"

"Jasper!" she cried. "Welcome to the Earthly Realm!"

Jasper climbed out of the lake, and the two dragons clinched.

Jesse and Daisy stood around feeling happy for Emmy and Jasper but also rather awkward. Jesse turned and invited Daisy to appreciate the way the sun was sinking down into the west.

"Like a broken egg yolk, spreading out along the horizon," Jesse said.

"Exactly!" said Daisy. "And speaking of which, I'm hungry. Emmy, can we please get going?"

Behind them, Emmy cleared her throat carefully. "Cousins, if you two don't mind," she said, "I think I'd like to stay here and give Jasper a chance to see his first sunset."

"I think that means she wants to be alone with him," Jesse whispered to Daisy.

"That's fine," Daisy whispered back to Jesse. "But that means no ride home for us. And it's a *long* way home."

Just then, they heard a familiar clopping sound. Jesse and Daisy whipped around to see Old Bub plodding up the side of the mountain.

"Your ride is here," Emmy said brightly.

"When will we see you back at the garage?" Jesse asked.

"Oh, no," said Emmy, frowning with sudden

vehemence, "you won't be seeing me in that stinky old garage ever again."

Daisy looked stricken. "We'll make improvements, we promise!" she said.

"Honest!" Jesse said.

"Face it, Keepers. I'm too big for the garage now. I'm thinking the barn is more my style."

"Great!" said the cousins, relieved that her new nest would be someplace nearby and as familiar and dear to them as their own home.

Emmy went on, "I'll stay in the barn part of the time and in my cottage in the Fiery Realm the other part of the time."

The cousins groaned.

"I like my cottage!" Emmy protested. "It's just the right size! I never bump my head on the ceiling, never have to be a sheepdog, and I have a very nice cozy nest there."

"Yeah, but it's so far away," Jesse said.

"And no offense, but I don't think either one of us is in any hurry to get back to the Fiery Realm," Daisy said, with a telling little shake of her newly enlivened left arm.

"And anyway, how are we supposed to know when you're going to show up in the barn?" Jesse said, trying very hard not to sound whiney.

"You'll know I'm in the barn when this happens," Emmy said, blinking her great green eyes.

Daisy let out a soft cry. She held up her left arm and pushed up the sleeve of her coat. "My arm tingles like crazy!" she said. "And look, Jess!"

Jesse gaped at the sight of his cousin's arm. Each of the hundreds of fine white hairs had a little tiny flame on it, just the way they had in the Fiery Realm. "Whoa," said Jesse. "Now *that* is an even cooler souvenir than your Purple Star and my Silver Heart."

"It sure is!" said Daisy, continuing to stare at her arm in astonishment.

"I mean," said Jesse, "that's what I call a genuine *fire arm!*"

Daisy lowered her arm, which had stopped tingling. "Well, I guess we'll run along now and leave you two lovebirds alone."

"No, no, no. Not lovebirds," said Emmy, shaking her head. "We are *like* birds, aren't we, Jasper?"

"As I always said," the big galoot murmured, "Emmy and I are boons."

"I'm way too young to have a fiery mote," Emmy said.

"Then what was all that fiery mote business about?" Jesse asked.

"St. George put a spell on Emmy that made her crave me for the fiery mote of her heart. St. George wanted to trap Emmy in the Fiery Realm, and he used me for bait," said Jasper with a sigh.

"What broke the spell?" Jesse asked.

"Maybe it broke when we came up through the crater lake," Daisy said. "Just like my arm got its feeling back, Emmy lost the fiery mote feeling for Jasper."

"And we're glad you did," Jesse said.

"I'll say!" said Daisy. "We should have known all along that you were too cool for school."

Old Bub snorted and pawed at the earth with a front hoof.

"I think he's trying to tell us something," said Daisy.

Old Bub pawed again, as if to say, *Enough talk. Let's get going.*

"We have to get home," Jesse said. "School tomorrow."

After Daisy and Jesse said their so-longs to the two dragons, Emmy boosted them onto Old Bub's back and gave the horse's flank a friendly smack to send him on his way. Daisy gripped Jesse around the middle with both hands, and Jesse clung to Old Bub's mane.

As Old Bub started down the mountainside,

Jesse wondered aloud, "So how do you think the new twins are doing? Do you think Cousin Paul liked the card I made him? I wonder what Miss Alodie's been up to while we've been gone. I hope Teachers' Conference Day went well. Do you think Ms. Lasky learned lots of neat new teaching tricks?"

To which Daisy responded in her best Flaminian style: "Desist with the dithering details, earthly upstart!"

They both enjoyed a good chuckle as Old Bub plodded all the way back to the barn.

The sun had set by the time they arrived at the old barn doors. As soon as they slipped off Old Bub's back, he gave a sigh and slowly faded into the twilight, leaving only the four rusty horseshoes. Jesse and Daisy returned the horseshoes to the Museum of Magic, where they also placed the Purple Star and the Silver Heart, next to the Toilet Glass. Now that the Witch of Uffington was no longer trapped inside it, they were altogether more comfortable about having it there.

When Jesse and Daisy crawled through the tunnel in the laurel bushes and poked their heads out, they saw a bonfire burning in their own backyard.

"It's like the Fiery Realm followed us home,"

said Jesse as they kicked their way toward it through the fallen leaves.

Daisy started to sing, and soon Jesse joined in:

> *"Fire's burning! Fire's burning!*
> *Draw nearer! Draw nearer!*
> *In the gloaming! In the gloaming!*
> *Come sing and be merry!"*

Miss Alodie was hunkered down next to the fire. She was roasting something over it on long sticks.

"Miss Alodie, cooking completely normal food? Hot dogs and buns?" Jesse said. "Who would have thunk it?"

"Hail, cousins!" Miss Alodie called out when she saw them. "As you can see, I have kept the home fires burning. You're just in time for a soy wiener roast."

"I should have known she wouldn't cook *real* hot dogs," Jesse said with a snort.

"You kids are looking mighty peckish!" Miss Alodie said.

"Are you kidding? We're *starved!*" said Daisy. "We've pretty much been living on air for the past few days."

"Well, I want to hear all about it," said Miss

Alodie, her blue eyes twinkling in the firelight.

"Hey, look!" Daisy said, pointing into the depths of the fire.

"Oh, yeah!" said Jesse, seeing it, too. There in the fire, side by side, were a little orange point like the fire on a birthday candle, a small flame flickering—white one moment and blue the next— and a small, round, red burning ball that looked extremely pleased with itself.

"Hey, you three!" said Jesse, waving to the fire fairies. "I hope you guys don't get in trouble for all licking through at the same time."

"Are you kidding?" Daisy said with a laugh. "Those little guys *are* trouble."

Later that night, Jesse got on his computer and typed a note to his parents.

Dear Mom and Dad, Daisy and I had a great three-day weekend. The bad news is that our dog, Emmy, ran away. The good news is that we tracked her down. We have decided to let her live on a farm nearby. It's for the best. She wasn't happy in the garage. On the farm there is lots of room for her to run around and play. We discovered why she ran away. She met a friend named Jasper. Jasper is a

real galoot, sort of bronze-colored with a
long tail. He has a very good heart. He and
Emmy are now good buddies. Daisy and I are
planning to visit Emmy in her new home as
often as we can. We also did some research
for our science fair projects. Daisy got a lot
of data on gemstones. And you will be happy
to know that I have a topic. Can you guess
what it is? It's volcanoes! And I have to say,
I am really *on fire* with ideas.

Your son in the Earthly Realm,

Jesse Tiger

KATE KLIMO drew the inspiration for *The Dragon in the Volcano* from a volcano and a gigantic horseshoe.

The volcano came from a vacation in Italy, where she stayed in a hotel under the shadow of Mount Etna in Sicily. From her balcony she could see sparks and smoke—like the fiery breath of a dragon—rising from the peak every night.

Kate dug up the gigantic horseshoe near her new home in New Paltz, New York. It was the biggest horseshoe she had ever seen, and she couldn't help but imagine what sort of horse would wear such a shoe, and thus Old Bub was created.

Kate lives with her husband, Harry, and a carnivorous cat named Pretty Kitty. They have two (normal-size) horses that they ride whenever they can.